WHEN THE VOWS BREAK

A Novel by
Janie De Coster

To submit a manuscript for our review, email us at

submissions@majorkeypublishing.com

Be sure to <u>LIKE</u> our Major Key Publishing

page on Facebook!

There is a way that seems
right to a man but
in the end it leads to death

Proverbs 10:25

Or what shall a man
give in exchange for his soul
Mark 8:37

PROLOGUE – THREE YEARS AGO

Pastor Sidney Teal leaned back in his leather office chair and regarded the young man seated before him with a mixture of compassion and sternness. Sylvester Goodings had been a member of Holy Word Holiness Church from the time he'd been a hard-headed little boy who gave Sister Duncan fits when she was the Sunday school teacher. Now in his late twenties, that hard head had been replaced with the respectful, hard-working, and married Brother Goodings.

However, that wasn't the man in front of Pastor Teal right now. That man was filled with remorse and shame.

"I love Dana, Pastor Teal. The Lord above knows I do. She's been my rock through it all, and I'd never do anything to hurt her. It's just that—that—I get weak. I pray and pray and promise to myself that I won't do it again, and for a while, things are fine. Then—"

Sidney folded his hands in front of him. Yes, this was a time for compassion but also time for a mild rebuke. He'd heard gossip around the church about Brother Goodings messing around, but he gave no credence to it, having seen how devoted the young man was to his beautiful wife, Dana.

"This last time, Dana found out, and I told her everything. Now she's threatening to leave me."

Sylvester's voice was thick with pain.

"I know she dealt with that from her father, and she had a hard time trusting me, but dammit, Pastor Teal, I went and did the same thing. I let her down, but I let myself down, and I disobeyed God. I thought I was a better man than that."

Pastor Sidney Teal leaned forward, his warm brown gaze direct and uncompromising.

"There is no better man than Jesus, Brother Goodings. The rest of us fall far short of His grace. However, because He gave his life for us, we can find forgiveness and a chance to be better men."

"Amen," Sylvester intoned quietly.

"Brother Goodings, I'm going to tell you what I tell everybody who comes to me with this sin on their souls. And believe me, son, you'd be surprised at how many Holy Word members have found themselves led into temptation."

He took a deep breath.

"Brother Goodings, avoiding temptation, especially of the flesh, has never been an easy task. Think about it—all

9

these young girls running around in next to nothing, copying what they see on TV. You'd think they all shopped at Strippers 'R' Us or something. Sadly, a lot of them don't know any better, confuse sex with love, and get led astray by some man, but that's no excuse. The Lord gave us five senses so that we know right from wrong, and the fact is that I don't care if a woman is butt naked and begging. When you give your word to the Lord and when you speak your vows, you've got to do everything in your power to keep them. Am I right?"

"Yes, Pastor Teal. I know all that, but—"

"But *nothing*, my young brother. Who you gonna follow, the Lord or the world?"

Sylvester hung his head down, contrite.

"Yes, Pastor Teal, I know. I gave my life to the Lord, and that's all there is."

The older man stood up, walked around his desk, and placed a gentle hand on the other man's shoulder.

"The good news, Brother Goodings, is that forgiveness is yours for the asking. The fact is that you're here, and that means you want the Lord to change your heart."

He felt Brother Goodings tremble underneath him, trying to not cry.

"Trust me, son. Every man is tested and sometimes finds himself wanting. Believe me. As a man who has vowed to serve the Lord, the enemy is always looking to challenge me."

He gave Brother Goodings a tissue.

"My wife and I have been married nearly fourteen years, and I have never strayed. You've got to know that the temptations are great."

"How do you do it, Pastor Teal?"

"It's called self-control, son, and thinking with the head on your shoulders and not with that one between your legs."

He chuckled.

"I know the older members of the congregation would be scandalized to hear me talk that way, but I found that when I talk to young folks, I have to speak their language. You know what I'm saying?"

Brother Goodings nodded again.

"You have to keep the commitment you made to your wife in the center of your mind, and even take yourself away from those who would lead you astray, even if they're your friends. Keep in mind the fourth chapter, verse seven of James. 'Submit yourselves therefore to God. Resist the devil, and he will flee from you.'"

"Yes, Pastor Teal. I just want my Dana to forgive me and for us to start over again."

Sidney sat on the edge of the desk, his expression kind.

"I can't promise you that, my young brother. Dana is a strong young sister, and she demands respect. I will call her to schedule a session with her as well and hope that in time she'll see the good in you and want to start over. You just have to pray on it, and show her that you are truly remorseful. Make her feel like the queen that she is. Shower her with gifts, listen to her every word, and understand that her trust in you has been shattered and that while it may take some time to repair, all things are possible when you trust in the Lord."

Sidney extended his hand to Brother Goodings. The younger man stood, shook Sidney's hand firmly, and then reached out to hug him. Sidney gave him a comradely pat on the back.

"I'm going to do all I can to show the Lord that I'm a better man, and I will get my wife back," Sylvester declared with determination as he made his way to the door. Sidney didn't doubt Brother Gooding's sincerity.

"I'll be praying for you and Dana too. Us black folks need strong marriages and families to survive."

"Amen to that, Pastor Teal. And thank you."

Sidney waited until Brother Goodings' back had retreated down the hall before he closed the door of his study. Once the door was closed, he stretched his legs and worked the stiffness from his neck. He missed his wife, Olivia's, deft fingers that knew exactly how to soothe and heal his soul. Walking over to his desk again, he gathered up some notes he'd made before the counseling session and placed them in the drawer. His stomach growled rudely, reminding him that it was way past his lunch time and that he needed to head home. Retrieving the keys to his black Escalade, he took his signature brim from the stand and walked out.

It had taken twenty long and sometimes lean years before the Holy Word Holiness Church became what it was now, one of the largest churches in New York. Sidney took a little time to once again admire and praise the Lord for what had been wrought in his name; the high cathedral ceilings, cherry wood pews, and altar. The magenta and gold plush carpet sank beneath his Italian-made loafers. The stained-glass fixtures had been a gift from one of the talented young people who'd come to his church looking for peace away from the violent streets of her neighborhood, and the showpiece was the black Jesus with arms outstretched and a beatific expression on his face. While some members of his congregation took some offense at the depiction, most welcomed it and thought it suitable for a church that catered to a mainly African American fellowship. Holy Word could easily seat well over two thousand folks on any given day and often did.

At the end of the day, it was still a building. Holy Word's strength depended greatly on the people who came and on those who joined and made themselves a home. It also depended upon himself being a dynamic and charismatic minister who could sing Shirley Caesar and then get down with some Marvin or Luther. It was said he could preach and do stand-up comedy at the same time. He didn't do fire and brimstone very well, believing that scaring folks to Jesus only lasted as long as they were afraid.

On his way to the parking lot, he noticed Sister Margie Davis with a group of women from the planning committee talking near the recreational room. Tomorrow was the Holy Word Holiness Youth Festival, and knowing how detail oriented Sister Margie was, they were probably making last minute arrangements.

They'd been having the youth festival for five years and brought hundreds of people from miles around. He'd heard that some folks actually flew themselves and their children to attend. Like Holy Word itself, the festival was a big event with plenty of food, including Jesse James Durham's world-championship barbeque, games, and other activities for both kids and adults. There would also be several youth choirs from neighboring churches as well as their own who would perform.

Yes, Pastor Teal thought proudly. Holy Word understood better than most that the youth was their future and that a strong sense of unity was key to the continuing success of black people.

As he approached, the women all stopped and greeted him with warm smiles from varying shades of brown faces.

"Checking up on us, Pastor?" Sister Margie asked jokingly with a wide grin.

"Don't you worry 'bout a thang like the song says. We've got it all covered."

Sidney didn't doubt that for a minute. Margie Davis had been in charge of youth activities at Holy Word for the past twelve years, and it was through her efforts that more young people became lifetime members of the church.

There was also a personal element to her devotion. As

15

a teacher and fairly recent divorcee with a thirteen-year-old son whom she kept a very short leash because she didn't want him getting caught up in the trappings of the gang life, she was passionate about giving the youth of her community other options in life besides crime and violence. Because she was such a strong and driven woman, her son, Jasper, was graduating high school and had been accepted at Howard University. In fact, nearly two hundred of Holy Word's high-school aged teens would be attending college the coming fall.

Sidney smiled back, revealing white and even teeth.

"And how are the rest of you ladies doing today, since Sister Margie has everything in hand?"

"We're just fine, Pastor Teal," they all chimed in unison. Some giggled or fluttered their lashes at him. He was used to that.

"Will you be coming to the festival tomorrow?" asked Vanessa Stacey, who was no more than fourteen or fifteen years but could have easily past for eighteen or nineteen, especially with the tight T-shirt she wore that was emblazoned with the logo of some urban fashion designer. Sidney sighed, remembering what he'd said to Brother Goodings earlier. Girls these days were far too well developed for their own good.

"Of course. Olivia and I will be there," he answered smoothly, knowing that naming his wife would quell any ideas some of the ladies might have had concerning his marital state.

"My children haven't talked about anything else nearly all week."

From the corner of his eye, he saw another young woman stride over to them as Sister Margie waved her over. He coughed, trying to hide his sudden discomfort. Her dark molasses skin glowed, set off perfectly by a fiery-colored form fitting sheath dress that accentuated every curve. Sidney took in her short but well-shaped legs that would have given Tina Turner a run for her money. Sidney's heart skipped a beat as the distance closed between them.

"Pastor Sidney, this is my niece, Yasmin Lewis," Sister Margie introduced proudly.

"She's planning to attend business school here and recently moved from South Carolina. I told her that I'd be getting her into this fine church the minute she arrived."

Yasmin extended a slender hand, and Sidney gently took it. Her skin felt like soft rose petals. The heady floral perfume she wore teased his nostrils.

"It's very nice to meet you, Pastor Teal. Auntie

17

Margie is always talking about you," Yasmin replied in a honey-sweet drawl. Her smile was warm, sincere, and almost innocently sexy. He didn't understand it. No other woman had affected him the way Yasmin Lewis had. In less than a minute, something had happened.

"Likewise, Miss Lewis," Sidney said, outwardly composed and inwardly a turbulent storm of emotion.

"Will you be at the youth festival tomorrow?"

Again, there was that innocent smile that he was reading far too much into.

"I sure will. I think what Auntie Margie is doing with the children is just wonderful, and I wish more churches would do the same."

Sidney couldn't help noticing the beam of approval from Sister Margie's eyes. He should rebuke her for the sin of pride, but he couldn't bring himself to say anything negative in front of her niece.

"Have you attended service yet?"

For some reason, he'd know if she had.

"I will this Sunday. I promise," she said, warm brown eyes smiling.

"Aunt Margie says you preach so good that you could get the devil to change his ways."

"Whatever," muttered Vanessa from the side,

obviously upset at being put in the shade. Sidney laughed.

"Oh, I don't know about all that. I just let the Lord fill me with His spirit, and the words just come. I don't take any credit for it."

"You're too modest, Pastor Sidney," added Sister Margie.

"Remember that article in *Ebony Magazine* about the One-Hundred Most Influential Ministers in America? You were number fifty-seven."

Yasmin's eyes widened.

"Oh my goodness. I saw that article when I was getting my hair done! That picture didn't do you justice."

Was the look in her eyes and her words sending him a silent message, or was it just his imagination running wild at the sight of the vivacious young woman? Before he made a bigger fool out of himself, Sidney graciously bowed.

"Ladies, I was on my way home for lunch. I hope to see you all tomorrow."

Especially you, Miss Yasmin Lewis, was the rest of the unspoken thought.

Once inside his SUV, he turned the air on full blast and closed his eyes. The divine vision of the woman he had just met came into sharp focus. Something about her intrigued him. She touched him in a way that made his whole body respond in a totally inappropriate manner. He couldn't wait to see her again.

Reaching down to switch off the air, his conscience raged at him. What in heaven's name was he *thinking*? Just minutes ago, he was counseling Brother Goodings about infidelity and giving in to temptation. He needed to take heed of his own advice and stay clear of Yasmin Lewis until he could make sense of his feelings.

CHAPTER ONE

Another trip out of city and the last one for a while, Sidney Teal hoped as he pulled into the multi-level parking structure adjacent to Holy Word Holiness Church. He allowed the engine of the Escalade to idle for a bit. Sometimes, he had to pinch himself to make sure he wasn't dreaming.

Holy Word was *his.* From a small-time storefront sanctuary to this luxurious and elegantly designed building with a packed congregation every Sunday, it was all *his* for the glory of the Lord.

Sidney walked into his personal office to drop off some brochures and check his mail. He'd just returned from a pastors' convention in Mississippi and was tired and drained. The seminar was very informative, and he'd gained knowledge that would help him further enhance his own ministry. Sidney smiled thinly at the thought of what else he had learned, trying to keep the images at bay and the attendant guilt underneath them.

She had accompanied him on this trip under the chaste guise of secretary—Yasmin. He'd even gone so far as to book separate rooms on different floors. As a secretary, she'd been more than efficient at transcribing his sermons and keeping his various appointments. It was her other talents that brought heat and shame.

In his heart of hearts, Sidney knew it was wrong. They both did. As a man of God, always counseling others through infidelity, he had absolutely no business doing what he did.

His only defense was simply that he couldn't help himself. At least that's what he told himself every time the guilt would overwhelm him.

To ease his guilty conscience, the only thing he could say was that after fourteen years of marriage, Yasmin Lewis was his first and only mistress. He could also say he'd been faithful to *her* for three years.

"Anybody home!" Sidney called out, entering the marble foyer of his elegant two-story home in an affluent section of the city. He removed his navy-blue Armani suit jacket, hung it upon the antique coat-tree, and walked into the empty living room.

The house was quiet and peaceful, decorated tastefully in creams and subtle earth tones. The walls were a showcase of the best African-American artists, including a few from the trips of their travels to other countries. His wife, Olivia, had an eye for style and firmly believed that only her elegance and expertise added value to their home.

Visitors to their home believed it was professionally done, and Olivia had received both compliments and commissions which she took before the children had come along. Now she was a full-time mother and preacher's wife, and Sidney had been pleased.

Their home had an exquisitely designed pool with a gazebo and a double garage which housed his black Escalade and Olivia's pearl white one. Sidney slid onto the couch and laid back, contentment in his pose. Yes, God had been more than very good to him. He was blessed with a lovely home, a beautiful wife, two energetic little boys who thought the world of him, and his precious little angel, Amia, who was only two and a half. He had a wonderful ministry that had grown beyond his expectations and had touched so many lives. So *why*?

The *why* was Yasmin Lewis. For years, there had been women in the church who'd thrown themselves at him. A few would invite him over to their homes, pretending to be broken-hearted over a failed romance or some other negative situation that happened in their lives, all the while dressing provocatively. His response then had been gentle chastisement mixed with kindness, and they, in turn, respected him for his refusal, but he couldn't or didn't want to refuse Yasmin.

The woman had him mesmerized the first time he saw her. She walked with an unconscious grace and presence as if she were royalty. Unlike those others, Yasmin hadn't sought his advances. She worked for the church, and she respected him. When she finally moved on in her career as a financial consultant in Downtown Manhattan, he was both pleased and supportive.

Somewhere along the way, that respect had turned into affection and then into something else. Now they were in way too deep. Sidney exhaled slowly as he thought of her. He knew at some point he had to end it for both of their sakes.

"Welcome back, Sidney. How was the conference?"

Olivia Teal leaned down and planted an absent kiss on his cheek. The scent of Stella McCartney wafted through his brain. Like everything else about her, Olivia's fragrance was subtle and conservative. She was a very attractive woman but reserved. Not one for outward signs of wealth, she preferred classically tailored looks that showed off her still youthful body to her best advantage.

"It went well. I saw Pastor Hawkins from First A.M.E. He looked pretty good for somebody who just found out that his associate pastor had been dipping into the tithes. That's going to be an ugly situation, considering."

"Oh," she said. That was it.

"By the way, you haven't forgotten that we're taking the children to Coney Island tomorrow, have you?"

From her tone, it was obvious that Olivia thought he *had* forgotten.

With a thin smile, he replied, "No, Livvy, I haven't forgotten."

"That's good. That's all those kids have been talking about for the past few days."

Olivia sighed theatrically.

"If I hear one more 'whee,' they're grounded."

When he didn't respond, she began walking away.

"I'm going to pick up Little Sidney from practice. I didn't make anything for dinner, but I can pick up some Chinese if you want."

Sidney nodded absently, his eyes closed. He heard the clicking sound of her expensive heels and then the slamming of the door. He listened until he heard the sound of Olivia's SUV leaving the driveway. Then he took out his cell phone. Four rings later, he got the voicemail.

"Baby, I'm sorry, but I've got plans tomorrow, so I won't be able to come over."

The phone picked up.

"Why am I not surprised?"

There was disappointment and resignation in Yasmin's voice. He heard her sigh.

"Oh well. I knew what I was getting into."

Sidney's heart dropped. He hated making Yasmin sad.

"Well, we did have a few days together. Right, baby?"

"Yeah."

She sounded less than convinced.

"Look, I just got in the house and I'm tired. I'll see you in church on Sunday."

The phone clicked off.

CHAPTER TWO

Yasmin hung up the phone before Sidney could try to sweet talk his way back. It wouldn't take much to forgive that rich honeyed voice that could preach a fiery sermon on one hand and then talk sweet and low to her on the other.

Yasmin Lewis knew better than to have gotten involved with a married man. The fact that the married man was also her *pastor* sounded like one of those Lifetime movies her sister-girl, April-Rose, was always watching. She never thought in a million years she'd be living one, though.

Sure, she had admired the almighty Pastor Sidney Teal when she first met him. Who wouldn't? He was handsome, charismatic, and more importantly, a man of ambition and drive. He made it clear that everything he did, from the Youth Ministry to his Second-Chance Parolee Program was because and through the word of the Lord. It made her wonder if putting them together in this way was the Lord's will as a test. If so, she flunked dramatically with flying colors.

April-Rose told her over and over again, "You could do better than messing around with a married man, and a preacher one at that."

Like every mistress before her and after her, she knew that. But knowing didn't stop anything. She wasn't naïve. She didn't think that he'd ever leave his wife and kids, much less jeopardize his honorable position in the church.

It wasn't as if she didn't have what it took to attract a man. Every time she and April-Rose went out, men of all races found her to their liking. She took a certain amount of pride in her appearance and held herself with grace and elegance. Her dark brown skin was ageless and kept a lot of people guessing. Every two weeks, she went to the same hair salon where Oprah's stylist often paid a visit, and dropped several bills on services and products to keep her locks straight and silky. No weaves or lace-fronts for Yasmin; she'd been blessed with a nice grade of long hair.

Working out four times a week, including Pilates, kept her body slim and fit with just the right amount of curves that made everything she wore look perfectly tailored.

She had a great job at Wheatley & Dunn, one of the largest corporate financial consulting firms in the country. Her two-bedroom condo was less than a year away from being paid for, and she vacationed every year in some exotic locale. Yasmin was doing so well, in fact, that with her last bonus, she went out and bought a brand new Lexus 35i as well as a brand new wardrobe, including three pairs of Christian Louboutins.

Sidney was always talking about taking care of her, but Yasmin was no gold digger. She could do bad all by herself, and as you could see, she wasn't.

It should have been a one-time thing only. That's what she'd told herself that first night they'd crossed the line. The sex had been off the damn chain. She had to admit that. Sidney Teal might have been a man of God, but when he first put it on her, Yasmin swore she saw heavenly angels and heard the sound of the trumpet as she reached her peak. The preacher man had skills and had her feeling so damn good that she would have slapped her mama had he told her to. All he requested from her was her fidelity, and of course, her discretion.

From her point of view, Yasmin believed the liaison between them had been a moment of weakness. Now, after years had passed, she was still weak. It had been so stupid of her to have gone out of town with him for the pastors' convention, stupid to have dined with him under the pretense of church-related matters, and even stupider to have gone back to his room.

Hell, Yasmin thought disgustedly, *I didn't even enjoy the sex this time.* In her pretense, she'd made all the right sounds as if he was pushing all her buttons, but inside, she just wanted it to be over. If she were honest, she was glad that he called to cancel. Tonight, she'd have a long hot soak with a bottle of Moet and some Coltrane in the background.

***

Olivia sped off, needing to put distance between her and Sidney.

"He must think I'm three kinds of fool," she muttered over the sounds of Jill Scott from the CD player.

Olivia Teal was certain her marriage was on its last leg. Oh, they'd stay together for the sake of the kids and to present a united front for his congregation, but as far as she was concerned, the whole mess was becoming harder to maintain.

Sidney was having an affair. The signs were obvious. Thankfully, whoever the bitch was, she knew how to be discreet. There were a lot of women at Holy Word who had no shame in their game and would make a point of letting everyone in the church know it. Long before this, women had thrown themselves at her husband. Some still did, and the ring on his finger just meant a challenge. The few friends she'd mentioned her suspicions to were no help at all. Cynthia Casey, the wife of one of his deacons and supposedly her best friend, couldn't understand why Olivia was so upset.

"Girl, you're living in a million-dollar home, driving an expensive luxury car, and have enough clothes to start your own store. Why go messin' that up 'cause he might have a little something on the side? Men are dogs, even holy ones. You know that."

Olivia wanted to slap some sense into Cynthia, but she figured that not inviting her to the annual Women's Baptist Auxiliary Retreat in Palm Beach in the fall was revenge enough.

Olivia was patient. She'd bide her time until the man slipped up, then take everything she was entitled to. The mega church, he could keep. That is… if his congregation would still want his cheating ass after the shit hit the fan.

***

Ring! Ring! Ring!

The long soak had done its magic. Yasmin had slept like a baby through the night. The phone rang again. She turned over and looked at the clock on the nightstand. *8:00 a.m.* Whoever it was didn't understand it was Saturday morning, and she hadn't had her coffee yet. She

31

picked it up and managed to groan out a sleep-filled, "Hello?"

"Hey, sister girl!" April-Rose's voice boomed over the phone. Her BFF had no sense of timing.

"Do you know what time it is? No one gets up this early on a Saturday, at least no one with an ounce of sense."

"You ain't got a man over there, so get your ass up," she said with a chuckle in her voice.

"You know this is our shopping and spa day, and I saw the hottest Dooney & Bourke bag over at Sak's. It's got my name written all over it."

Then she went quiet.

"Don't tell me *Preacher Man* is over there."

April-Rose didn't like Pastor Teal and never missed a moment to say so. She also refused to call him by name, choosing instead to call him 'Preacher Man.'

"No. He called yesterday to cancel our plans. I guess it's family day or something."

Yasmin tried to sound light about it, but her friend knew her too well. She was upset.

"Look, Yaz. I try to stay out of your business, but you've got to kick Pastor Playa to the curb. I don't get you, girl. Everywhere we go, men are always trying to get at you. You work with some fine ass brothas at that firm of yours. You really don't need to be some man's bit of chocolate dessert on the side."

Yasmin didn't want to discuss her love life this early in the morning, even with her BFF.

"I'm so not in the mood for this shit. If you're gonna start this mess, you can go shopping by yourself."

"Okay, okay. I've said my piece. Now get up, get dressed, and I'll pick you up in an hour. And I don't mean CP time either," April-Rose added, knowing Yasmin had a tendency to be late.

"I'll even treat you to breakfast. Plus, I've made appointments for us at Bliss."

Yasmin stretched and swung her legs over the side of the queen-sized bed, still holding the phone to her ear.

"Can't turn down free food."

She sighed, getting a little excited about their day. She looked down at her feet and wrinkled her nose. *Ooh, and my feet are so whacked. I could use a pedicure. I want one of those Minx pedicures that I saw Beyoncé with. It'll look good with those Jimmy Choos I bought,* she thought happily.

CHAPTER THREE

The boys came bursting into the bedroom as Sidney and Olivia slowly opened their eyes.

"C'mon, daddy. Wake up," Sidney Jr. barked as he pounced on his father's broad chest like a frisky cat. Sidney gasped from the weight of the pint-sized dynamo as he propped himself up.

"Daddy, Mommy, wake up, please!" Joshua pleaded in his small voice.

"We're going to Coney Island today, and we don't wanna be late!"

Sidney Jr. was the oldest at seven, and he was the carbon copy of his father, whereas Joshua at five had his mother's light complexion. Sidney grabbed his young son, flipped him onto his back, and began to tickle him until the boy squirmed. Olivia watched with wry amusement in her eyes. Her husband might not have felt much for her these days, but he was a good father. She was willing to work something out with him in regard to custody. After all, boys needed their father, though it would be somewhat ironic for Sidney to teach them what being a man was all about, considering.

"Alright, you guys, I'm up." Sidney managed to chuckle.

"Go wake up Amia and get ready."

"Yes, Daddy," both boys chorused then scrambled from the room to grab their baby sister. Sidney yawned and stretched. His eyes met Olivia's. She looked at him with a knowing smile that was far from the smiles she used to give him.

"I'll go get ready," she said abruptly as she slipped from beneath the sheets. The kiss she gave him on the lips was cool, as if it were a duty and not something that used to lead to being late for social functions.

"It will be nice to spend time with the kids and you," Sidney added lightly. She padded off to the bathroom in a haze of peach-colored silk, never looking back once to see if he was planning to follow. At one point in time, he would have.

Sidney sighed and sank back into the bed, staring up at the ceiling. He knew the distance between them was his doing. He'd long suspected that Olivia knew he was having an affair, but for her own reasons, chose to ignore it—and him. Perhaps, she did it because of the children. Family was as important to her as it was to him, but for vastly different reasons.

He reflected on his own upbringing. His father never took them anywhere, not even to a simple ball game. Sidney had promised himself if he ever had a family that things would be different, and they were, until his indiscretion.

Olivia shrugged out of her satin gown and let the material flutter to the floor. She gave her still toned and youthful body a quick once over, satisfied with what she saw: nice hips, full and heavy breasts, and a nice ass. She took pains to keep herself looking good, but it hadn't kept Sidney out of some other bitch's hole. She chuckled darkly, remembering his frivolous attempts at lovemaking last night, like she wanted him anywhere near her. Who the hell knew what kind of diseases he brought back home from the whore he was seeing? The church had recently had a seminar on HIV and the black community and how it was important to get tested. Wouldn't that be something if she insisted Pastor Sidney get tested?

Olivia stepped into the marble shower stall and let the water and expensive bath gel reinvigorate her senses. She hoped Sidney had enough sense to use the other bathroom. Another encounter was something she didn't want.

***

. Yasmin and April-Rose came away from their spa and shopping day shiny, happy, and with their slender arms full of bags. As they were putting them in the trunk of April-Rose's silver Mustang, her cell phone rang. Yasmin slid into the passenger seat, adjusted the straps of her spaghetti-strap sundress, and closed the door against the ninety-degree heat.

"That was Ronnie," April-Rose told her as she slid into the driver's side and started up the engine.

"Damn, it's hot out there."

She reached for the air conditioner, turning it up full blast.

"He was wondering if you wanted to hang out with us later."

"What's up?"

"He wants to go to Coney Island," she said, rolling her eyes heavenward with a chuckle.

"He's such a big kid. Actually, his cousin, Ambrose, just came from L.A., and I guess he wants to show him a good time."

Yasmin raised an eyebrow.

"At Coney Island in the middle of *this* heat? Don't you know chocolate melts?"

"So you don't want to go?"

"I didn't say that."

"Does it have anything to do with preacher man?"

Yasmin sucked in a breath.

"Don't start with me, girl."

"Someone needs to," April-Rose retorted.

"Better me than his wife going all Jerry Springer on your ass."

Yasmin rolled her eyes.

"So tell me about Ronnie's cousin, Ambrose," Yasmin said, instantly switching topics. So far, their day was going great, and she didn't want to ruin it with another fight over Sidney.

"He's a real estate attorney at some big-time firm in Downtown L.A. Nice car, nice townhouse in Brentwood, dresses to the nines, and isn't gay or dating a white woman," April-Rose quipped.

"Oh, and he surfs."

Yasmin's eyes widened in disbelief.

"You're kidding, right? And he's Ronnie's *cousin*?"

April-Rose chuckled.

"Okay, so he's not your typical brother, but he's got it going on where it counts, and he's *single*," she emphasized.

"But Ronnie says he just got out of a relationship with some ghetto princess who had a little thug life on the side."

"So you already met him before?"

"We met last summer when he came for a short visit."

April-Rose could read the expression on her best friend's face.

"And before you get mad at me, I didn't introduce you two because your head was so buried in Preacher Man that you wouldn't have seen your behind if it wasn't attached to you."

Yasmin's mind drifted back to last summer and realized April-Rose was right.

"Yeah, but you still could have mentioned him to me."

She pouted.

"I could have kicked Sidney to the curb a long time ago."

"Oh yeah, like you would have been *real* interested in meeting him."

April-Rose sighed in disbelief. The drive continued in silence, except for the John Legend CD in the background. Both women were lost in their own thoughts. Driving always helped April-Rose think, and she was thinking deeply about her best friend. There were few women of any color April-Rose Thomas could stand to be around for long periods of time because, as she put it, she *watched* drama. She didn't want to be in the middle of it. From past experiences, most of her girlfriends tended to have a lot of drama, usually of the baby daddy variety.

That was why none of what Yaz was doing made any sense, unless sex with preacher man was all that and a bag of french fries. True, good sex could make a girl's head spin, but sooner or later, the ride had to end. Yaz was smart, had looks, her own money, her own car, and an apartment. In short, she was, as Destiny's Child called it, an independent woman. She should have been the very last woman in the world desperate for a man.

The Mustang pulled up to Yasmin's building. They got out of the car and began pulling her bags out of the trunk. April-Rose grabbed her friend's hand.

"You're my girl, Yaz, and I don't like to see you getting all twisted over him. You deserve so much better."

Yasmin nodded slowly and sighed.

"I know that."

"Sweetie, it's past time you let Preacher Man go. He can't do anything for you, except make you miserable."

41

"I know. Maybe I'm just sprung."

"Well, girl, let's see what we can do to get you *un-*sprung."

***

The kids were having the time of their lives; Sidney Jr. with Joshua in tow, sometimes getting away from them in their excitement. Sidney and Olivia strolled through the crowd with two-and-a-half-year-old Amia in her Jeep tri-stroller. For all intents and purposes, they were the perfect family and the perfect high-class couple. It was all an act, but for the sake of the kids, both played their parts to the hilt.

"Daddy, can we have something to drink?" Sidney Jr. asked, wiping the sweat from his little forehead as he struggled to hold onto the big stuffed Dalmatian Sidney had won him for him in the basketball toss.

"How 'bout some lemonade?" he asked as he steered them all to the closest stand.

"Yay! I want a big one," announced Joshua, holding his SpongeBob Square Pants stuffed figure by its leg.

"You always spill yours. Then you want some of mine," Sidney Jr. said. The brothers cheerfully squabbled as they moved toward the vacant picnic tables by a waterfall. The cool mist refreshed them, comforting them in the simmering summer heat.

"Having a good time?" Sidney asked Olivia, debating whether he should attempt to hold her hand. She looked very pretty in a white flowing cotton sundress. She smiled, but the warmth didn't reach her eyes.

"Of course. It's nice to do something with our kids *together*," she replied, emphasizing the last word.

"You're right, honey."

Sidney lowered his eyes as he sucked up the last of his lemonade. He got her message loud and clear.

"I'm having lots of fun, Mommy," Joshua squealed, breaking the tension between them as he sat on his father's lap.

"Me too!"

Sidney smiled, reaching down to tickle baby Amia in her stroller who pointed in the direction of the Ferris wheel.

"Ride that," she said as only two-year-olds could. Everybody laughed.

"Okay, you guys. We've got a lot more things to see and do, so stay with us, okay?" Olivia commanded as she grabbed ahold of the stroller.

CHAPTER FOUR

When the doorbell rang, Yasmin was adding a touch of lipstick to her full mouth. She wasn't nervous, but it had been a long time since she'd met a man who wasn't Sidney, and her heart was racing. It was stupid to be acting like she was being unfaithful. Sidney had no right to have claims on her. *He* was the one cheating on his wife. It was absurd for him to demand fidelity. It was time to move on.

April-Rose opened the door, and two men stepped inside.

"Hey, sweetheart," Ronnie said, sweeping his lady up in a huge hug.

"I hope you're ready for some fun tonight."

Ronnie Stanton was tall with dark brown skin the shade of fresh-brewed coffee. His hazel eyes were surrounded by long lashes that any woman would kill for, and his open ready smile gave him the look of an eager college boy. She gave him a quick kiss.

"I am. Hopefully, it'll be much cooler down by the water, 'cause Yaz and I almost melted today."

Ronnie looked up and grinned at Yasmin.

"Hey, Yaz. Where you been keeping yourself these days?"

"Oh well, you know how it is in the consulting business. Tryin' to make those hours so that I can make my bills," she said. He gave her a quick brotherly hug.

"I feel ya, girl. I feel ya."

He released her.

"Oh, forgive my manners," he said, pointing to the figure behind him.

"This is my cousin, Ambrose Hunter, from L.A. He's here to see how we do things in the NYC."

Day-um was all Yasmin's mind could process. Ambrose Hunter easily *out-Tysoned* Tyson Beckford, and that was saying something. Look up the words tall, dark, and handsome, and the man standing in front of her would be in the dictionary. He looked less like a stuffy attorney and more like a man who belonged in GQ. His hair was close-cropped, and his face was smooth as a baby's bottom except for a slight mustache that framed his full lips when he smiled. He took her hand and shook it gently.

"Nice to meet you, Yasmin."

His voice was as rich and smooth as caramel, proper, and educated. He didn't seem the type to care if people thought it strange.

"Actually, it was my turn to come to the East Coast since Ronnie just recently visited me for my birthday."

"And I'll never do that again," Ronnie teased.

"Can you believe this fool tried to get me on a surf board? I wasn't trying to be shark food."

Yasmin just stood there, taking in the hotness that was Ambrose Hunter, all thoughts of Sidney Teal gone. She knew she'd turned the air on, but Yasmin was suddenly very warm. She wasn't even paying attention to the back and forth joking between the men until April-Rose grabbed her by the upper arm and steered her toward the spare bedroom.

"Won't be long, guys! Just need to grab some stuff!" she shouted from down the hall.

They rode in Ronnie's black Explorer—April-Rose sitting in the front and talking a mile a minute as she held her boyfriend's hand.

Wouldn't it just figure, Yasmin thought darkly as she rode in silence. *I'm introduced to the man of my dreams, and I'm stuck with some woman's sloppy seconds.* Ambrose was quite possibly the most perfect example of a BMW—Black Man Working. Hell, she could learn to like California in spite of the earthquakes. *What the hell is wrong with you?* she asked herself. *It's complicated between you and Sidney, so let it go, and enjoy this brother's company.*

Ambrose noticed his companion was distracted and wondered if he was the cause. She was a beautiful woman, but there was something different about her beauty. It was really sort of quiet and understated. In L.A., most of the women who flirted with him advertised their charms loud and clear.

"I'm not boring you, am I?" Ambrose asked, freeing Yasmin from her dark thoughts.

"It's the heat, I think," Yasmin replied, pretending to fan herself, though the air conditioning was on high.

"So, do you really surf?"

He grinned.

"You have a problem with that?"

"No, I've just never met any black folks who do… at least not around here," she quickly added, hoping that she didn't just screw up. Ambrose shrugged.

"No, that's okay. I'm kind of used to that sort of reaction. Ronnie gives me grief about it every time he calls me."

Yasmin sighed.

"I'm sorry. I must come off like some hood rat or something. Here I am, an educated black woman, and I just showed my ignorance."

"Actually, it's me who should apologize. I guess I get defensive about it for the wrong reasons. I just hate having to explain why I enjoy the sport and feel that I'm defending my blackness at the same time."

Yasmin nodded in understanding.

"I deal with that in the corporate world, so I feel you. So, what's it like?"

"You really want to know?"

"I do. Who knows? I might be inspired to try it someday."

Yasmin tried not to gasp as Ambrose's flawless face lit up. The man was more than just fine. She'd have a hard time keeping her composure being around him.

"Then you'll just have to come out to California and try it," he teased, showing a slight dimple in his chin that she'd missed back at the apartment.

"There's really no way to describe the feeling of riding the perfect wave."

"Uh oh," came Ronnie's rejoinder.

"Watch out, Yaz. He's gonna start getting all poetic about the sun and the waves and the sand and all that stuff. He doesn't talk about Jaws swimming around out there, looking for some soul food."

Everybody laughed, and Yasmin finally decided that she wasn't going to spare another wasted thought on Sidney. As a matter of fact, as soon as she got home, she was going to start a new chapter in her life, a chapter *minus* Sidney. Besides, there was a very hot piece of chocolaty goodness sitting right next to her who was willing to give her his undivided attention, and she was very interested in Ambrose Hunter.

April-Rose and Ronnie are definitely two of a kind, thought Yasmin as they stood in line for Ronnie's favorite rollercoaster, The Cyclone. The two of them were thrill junkies, whereas Yasmin preferred her rides to be a lot less terrifying. She wasn't timid by any means, but when it came to things that went up and down or upside down, they just weren't her cup of tea.

But here she was, standing next to Ambrose, getting ready to be strapped into a flimsy-looking set of cars that looked as if they'd not been repaired in fifty years. She tried her best to cover up her nervousness as they entered the loading gate.

The other two looked like kids in a candy store, eyes wide and excited.

"Hey, Yaz. You ready to go!" Ronnie whooped as the train came to a complete stop in front of them.

"Yeah, but this damn ride better not mess up my hair," she retorted.

"I spent a lot on this 'do."

Ambrose grinned with white teeth against perfect dark skin, and Yasmin's stomach did happy flip-flops. The man was *fine* with a capital FINE! She just couldn't get over it. Most blind dates bombed. What a lucky girl she was.

"I think your hair will be just fine, Yasmin," he said with an amused twinkle in his deep chocolate eyes.

"Roller coasters aren't that scary."

If you say so, she thought sourly as the cars began their slow trek upwards. Yasmin's heart beat frantically, and she wanted to kick herself in the butt for letting the three of them talk her into this. She promised herself that if she survived this, she'd get even with all of them.

"You better hang on to her as tight as you can, Ambrose."

April-Rose chortled with glee.

"Yaz may try to go suicidal!"

Before Yasmin could make a nasty comeback, the world seemed to tilt downwards, and she held on to the ride bar for dear life. She closed her eyes as she heard others screaming with laughter. She was screaming in sheer terror as the train banked quickly around the steep curves.

She wasn't aware of the moment Ambrose's fingers closed over hers, but she suddenly felt warm and safe. Suddenly, The Cyclone didn't seem as scary.

"You alright?" he mouthed over the rush of the wind. Yasmin nodded as she felt herself being lifted by gravity. Her eyes widened.

"Don't worry!" Ambrose shouted, grinning.

"They call that 'getting air.' That's what die-hard roller coaster fans live for."

They can have it, Yasmin thought as she felt she'd lose her stomach on yet another dip. Finally, the train clacked its way back into the loading station. Ronnie whooped like a little boy.

"Who wants to do it again?"

"Not hardly," Yasmin said, attempting to pat down her flyaway strands. Her voice was scratchy from all the screaming she did. Ambrose extended a hand to assist

Yasmin out of her seat. He was grinning like an idiot too. Yeah, they were related alright.

The rest of the afternoon slowly turned into a beautiful summer evening. The quartet rode other rides, though Ronnie and April-Rose took another turn on The Cyclone, leaving Yasmin and Ambrose to their own devices. They played carnival games and ate far too much.

While waiting for April-Rose and Ronnie to return, Ambrose regaled her with amusing stories about his life on the West Coast. For a man who had practically everything people would consider to be successful, he was incredibly humble. She liked that.

He was unlike any man she'd ever known. He traveled extensively, loved all sorts of foods, and was widely read. He was completely unlike Sidney: no wife, no kids, and no ties.

"I'm starvin'," Ronnie announced loudly, breaking their quiet conversation.

"You gotta be kidding. We just ate a couple of hours ago."

April-Rose sighed.

"That was hours ago," Ronnie shot back.

"We've done some serious ridin', and that makes me hungry."

April-Rose's hands went to her hips.

"I swear you must have a tapeworm somewhere in you," she mused as they followed him to the pizza parlor. They sat, ate pizza, and washed the thin-crusted slices down with a pitcher of ice-cold beer. The conversation flowed freely, and it seemed as if they'd all been hanging out like this for ages.

From the corner of his eye, Ronnie watched his cousin with Yasmin. He seemed to really be enjoying her company and vice-versa. That was a little unusual because Ambrose could be pretty reserved around people he didn't know, especially around some of Ronnie's friends who mocked his proper speech and California attitude. He was happy that his cousin was having a great time, but he was concerned too. Given what he'd already gone through, the last thing he wanted was for Ambrose to fall again for the wrong girl. Yasmin Lewis was as sweet as they came, but she had something going on that wasn't cool. A smart and intelligent woman like Yaz could do a hell of a lot better than messing around with a married man.

Both Ronnie and Ambrose had been raised with strict values from parents who didn't play. As a young man, he'd done his share of mess, but once he met his feisty April-Rose, he was committed. His friends said he was sprung, but that didn't bother him. At least he never had to deal with any baby mama drama.

April-Rose obviously wanted Yaz to meet someone just as handsome and successful as Sidney Teal but who wasn't married. Hopefully, the girl would kick Preacher Man to the curb and get on with her life before the whole thing blew up in her face. Ronnie knew church folks very well, and there was little doubt that it would.

As the sun slid toward the horizon, everyone was ready to call it a day, except for Ronnie, who just had to go on one more ride. It just had to be his all-time favorite, the water ride.

"Saving the best for last."

He chortled, smacking his girlfriend on the butt with the beach towel he'd stashed inside of April-Rose's big bag they had purchased from the gift shop. She grimaced, patting her hair gently.

"You do realize that if my hair gets wet, you're paying for another trip to the salon, right?"

Ronnie grinned like a little kid, ignoring his girl's statement.

"Ah man, this is gonna be fun! You guys ready!" he yelled back to Ambrose and Yasmin. Ambrose shrugged, shaking his head at his cousin.

"What do you say, Yasmin? Should we let him have all the fun?"

Yasmin broke into a million-watt smile at the sound of her name coming from Ambrose's lips. Suddenly, her high-maintenance hair didn't matter one bit. She would just flat-iron it in the morning.

Before she could stop herself, she grabbed his hand playfully and said, "Let's do the damn thing!"

***

"Are we done now?" April-Rose muttered jokingly while wringing the water from her long braids.

"I just hope you realize that I might have ruined a pair of leather gladiator sandals from BCBG for you."

Ronnie reached over and gave her a big kiss on the lips.

"And I appreciate it, baby," he replied with a wicked twinkle in his deep brown eyes. He glanced at his cousin.

"What about you, cuz? You ready to go?"

Before he had a chance to answer, April-Rose announced, "I need to visit the little girls' room."

"I'm right behind you, girlfriend," Yasmin chimed in, following her. Ronnie shook his head and sighed like every long-suffering boyfriend.

"I swear, man. They can never hold their water."

Ambrose spotted a basketball game booth and nudged his cousin toward it, saying, "You beat me the last time. I want revenge."

"Oh, hell yeah."

Ronnie laughed.

"Kobe versus LeBron. You're on!"

***

"So, what do you think of him?" April-Rose asked, rinsing her hands under the taps then reaching into her purse for her lipstick.

"He's nice," Yasmin responded nonchalantly as she peered into the mirror and re-applied her own lipstick.

"I'm still a little freaked out about the whole surfing thing. That's so weird."

"But you like him?"

She nodded.

"I think so. He doesn't come off with all that fake swag, and he's respectful."

"Damn, I'm good," April-Rose bragged loudly as two elderly white ladies entered the restroom and were momentarily taken aback. She smiled at them hugely.

"Don't worry, ladies. Me and my girl were just having a little conversation. She just found herself a single man. Whoo! Whoo!"

Yasmin held back the laugh in her throat as she looked into their bewildered faces. Sometimes, her best friend was a few cards short of a full deck.

Once outside, they spotted Ronnie who was holding a huge golden teddy bear.

"What the hell did you *do*?" April-Rose asked as Ronnie presented the stuffed animal along with another kiss.

"Black Mamba dominates again."

He chortled, looking straight at Ambrose.

"King James got *served*!"

Ambrose shrugged apologetically.

"He cheated."

"What? You just know the Lakers are the best, and you're from L.A."

"Oh hell."

April-Rose laughed.

"Let's go before they bore us to death with basketball talk. I already know I'm going to have to sit through NBA 2K on the PlayStation tonight."

Yasmin patted Ambrose on the hand, and her fingers tingled from the contact.

"It's okay, really. I'm not a big fan of stuffed animals anyway."

"Yeah right," her friend said while poking out her tongue at Yasmin.

They were leaving the amusement park, laughing and joking, when something made April-Rose glance up and around. She caught a glimpse of a familiar figure standing near a booth filled with toys and balloons. She maneuvered herself beside Yasmin, effectively blocking her friend's view. She wanted no drama here, not after the good time she'd been having with Ambrose.

Well, well. Looks like Sidney Teal was doing the good daddy thing, purchasing brightly colored balloons for his children. *How ironic*, she thought. The man was with his wife and kids, acting like the faithful husband and family man. She so wanted to shatter his little sanctified world, but she didn't want to hurt her best friend in the process.

April-Rose had seen Olivia Teal many times and could tell from a distance that she was a sister who didn't play. She was a strong-willed black woman who would probably sue her husband and take half, if not all, and then ask for more. Olivia Teal just didn't seem to be the *stand by your man* type that so many churches were full of.

She shivered. She had a feeling that none of this mess was going to end well for him or her best friend.

"I really enjoyed today."

Yasmin couldn't keep the wonder and the excitement from her voice as she looked at Ambrose.

"Even if a certain person almost made me lose my lunch on some damn rollercoaster."

Everyone in the car laughed, and the joy she felt was like a weight being lifted from her shoulders. It was so amazing to just be with a man without any drama. This was what her life ought to be, and hell, she was enjoying Ambrose's company. On the drive back, the two of them kept up a steady stream of conversation, and she found that she liked discussing things like art, books, and travel. Ambrose was well-traveled and regaled them all with tales about his various trips abroad, but Yasmin's mind was not fully at ease.

She felt strangely guilty, as if she was doing something wrong. She mentally shook her head, knowing damn well that April-Rose would bitch slap her for even thinking along those lines. In all the years she and Sidney had been messing around, she had never even looked at another man, much less had a date with one. Now as she took in the sight of Ambrose, who was as different from Sidney as any man could be, she realized just how much she was really missing out on.

He had all the qualities she had been searching for and thought wrongly that Sidney fit the bill. Ambrose was intelligent, ambitious, financially stable, and handsome. And the best part was that he was *free*.

She knew what she had to do. She knew when she checked her voicemail while her friend was in one of the stalls, that it had to end, starting tomorrow.

CHAPTER FIVE

It was a beautiful Sunday morning as Sidney prepared for his sermon. He glanced briefly at his notes, but his mind was still on yesterday. He'd thoroughly enjoyed being out with Olivia and the kids. Even she had been a little warmer than normal, allowing him to hold her hand and even steal a kiss or two. It seemed crazy that he had to do so, but Olivia hadn't been the demonstrative type for quite some time. Still, his children loved him, and they were the most important thing in his life. They saw Daddy, not the famous pastor whose face was as well-known as T.D. Jakes and Fred Price.

Sidney looked at the recently taken family portrait that graced the cover of a Christian magazine, which featured pastors and their families, and couldn't help but smile. In the photo, Sidney Jr. stood right beside him, looking like a miniature version of himself. Joshua, who had inherited his mother's light complexion, stood beside her, and Olivia, who was just as stunning as the day he married her, was holding Amia in her lap. Little Amia had the same dark eyes he possessed, with a dimple in her chin, just like his. God had definitely been good to him, and he should have been more than content. Any sane man would have.

There was a knock on the door of his study.

"It's me, Pastor Sidney," Deacon Ross's voice boomed from the other side of the door.

"Come on in!"

Sidney took a seat behind his mahogany desk, a huge smile on his lips. Deacon Ross Tindal was a big man, towering a little over six feet. He had played football during high school and college and had been scouted by the NFL. Unfortunately, a knee injury ended what many believed to have been a promising career, but Ross bounced back. He and his gorgeous wife, Chantel, started their own real estate business and were doing quite well for themselves. Ross fervently believed that when one door closed, another one opened.

"So, what's up, Sidney?"

Ross grinned, adjusting his navy-blue colored tie.

"The Lord has blessed us with another beautiful day."

"Yes, my brother. He has indeed. And as I'm just getting ready for services, I feel the spirit comin' on, ya feel me?"

The two of them had been friends since high school, though life had taken them down separate roads. Ross had been one of the original members of Holy Word when it was nothing more than another small storefront church like so many others. Nearly five years later, with the leadership of Sidney, they were now preaching the gospel in a million-dollar state of the art chapel. His congregation had swelled from a mere thirty-five members to almost three thousand at the latest count.

"I know we must be gaining at least a couple of hundred new members each month," Ross said with no small amount of pride.

"And yet, it still feels like that storefront church with the leaking pipes and the broken air conditioner. We still keep it real."

Sidney nodded.

"And that's why people come here, Deacon, 'cause we keep it real, giving them hope in this dismal world. Look at all the young people. Just last week, a couple of well-known gangbangers came in, and one fell down on his knees at the altar. Now he's a member. God is good."

"Amen, my brother," Ross echoed.

"Before long, we'll have this temple filled to the brim," Sidney declared as got up from behind his desk.

"So how are things going between you and Chantel? Are you two still working on that baby?" he asked playfully.

"We most certainly are; every night and every morning."

The other man grinned hugely.

"I want a family just like yours," he said as he picked up the portrait on Sidney's desk.

"It will happen to you one day, Ross. Just keep the good faith, and you know Olivia and I can't wait to be godparents," Sidney said, patting him on the shoulder.

"Oh, have you seen Deacon Miles this morning?"

Ross turned, headed for the door.

"Briefly. He was talking to Brother Alderman, the choir director.

"Okay, I'll talk to him later."

The other man nodded and walked out the door, leaving Sidney alone with his thoughts. He looked down at his sermon notes as he waited for the service to start, but his mind was on far more worldly and sinful matters. His mind kept floating back to Yasmin. He tried calling her a few times at the park when he was away from his family, but he kept getting her voicemail. He had no right to care whether or not she picked up the phone. Had no right to care what she was doing. She wasn't *his*.

He even tried last night after putting the kids to bed and while Olivia was on the phone with his mother, Clara. She was busy making arrangements to have his mother and his step-father, Melton, flown to New York for a visit.

"Why don't we pick your parents up from the airport and head over to Harlem for dinner?"

"That's fine, Livvy. Whatever you want," he replied absently as his mind wondered where in the hell Yasmin was. Olivia had stopped talking, glaring at him.

"I'm sorry, but am I *boring* you with these plans to entertain *your* family?" she asked caustically.

"No, sweetie. I'm so sorry."

Sidney attempted to be contrite.

"I was just thinking about poor Mrs. Witherspoon. Her husband was placed in a nursing home yesterday, and she's having difficulty accepting it. You know they've been together almost fifty-five years. It just brings great sadness to my heart."

Olivia nodded.

"Yes, I've forgotten how compassionate you are when it comes to your members. You treat everyone like they are part of your family," Olivia said, looking into her husband's face as if she could see right through him.

"The church is my family."

Sidney's mouth formed his words with a deep revelation.

"If it wasn't for them and the Almighty, we wouldn't be where we are now."

Sidney wasn't telling a complete lie to his wife. Beatrice Witherspoon's husband, Samuel, was indeed in a nursing home, but at that moment, they were the last thing on his mind. Yasmin Lewis was filling up all the space.

***

Sidney sat behind the fancy podium with Deacon Ross and Deacon Miles as he waited for the choir to bring the hymn "Amazing Grace" to a close. Within minutes, he heard his name being announced to the congregation, and he stood up proudly before the members of the Holy Word Holiness Church.

His black and gold robe shimmered in the light as he made his way to the podium. Sidney had another spiritual awakening as he looked out into the crowd. He could proudly state that his church was a true multicultural mix. It had often amazed him in the past how Sundays were often the most segregated day of the week. All God's children should worship together, and at Holy Word, they did. There were even a couple of Caucasians in the choir, and Lord could they sing, especially Bryan, who reminded Sidney of Eminem. The congregation was his flock. They depended upon him to give them direction, hope, and spiritual guidance. They clung to his every word as if he was their lifeline. Sidney was honored as well as humbled as he stood before them and delivered the good news. The bad news was that Yasmin was nowhere to be seen.

***

Sidney opened his leather-bound bible, notes scribbled in the margins and passages highlighted in green and yellow. It had been given to him several years ago on Father's Day by the Sunday school group, and though dog-eared, it was his favorite.

This morning's sermon was about peace, straight from Romans 12:9-21. There was no small irony about his choice, considering, but he was able to put everything aside as he began in his stentorian tone.

"If it is possible, as much as it depends on you, live peaceably with all men."

He glanced around his multi-racial church and asked, "Do you hear me?"

The voices answered in a fervent wave.

"Amen, Pastor Teal."

Their response slowly filled him, and he slowly raised his arms. He wasn't a shouting preacher. He preferred to talk and teach.

"You know the world we are living in today is in terrible condition. There is strife everywhere you look these days. You can't even turn on your television without hearing about some war going on somewhere. And my brothers and sisters…" his voice slowly raised as the congregation nodded.

"…the saddest thing about it all is there is just as much war and strife going on in our own homes as there are in the foreign countries of our world. Y'all know what I mean, church?"

The members nodded their heads, murmuring 'amen' in unison. Sidney picked up his white handkerchief and lightly patted his forehead. He stepped down from the podium and eased his way down into the audience.

"It's bad enough that we cannot do anything about the killing and the maiming that goes on all around us, but when we walk into the front door of our beautiful homes, we should be able to have serenity, calm, peace, and security. We should feel at peace in our own castles. Isn't that right, church?"

More 'amens' backed him up as he scanned the capacity of the crowd.

"After all, they say a man or a woman's home is their castle. Right, church?"

"Preach, brother!"

"Amen!"

"Tell the truth, Pastor Sidney!"

The congregation shouted their approval. Some clapped their hands as Pastor Sidney continued.

"A man or woman should be at peace with their spouses, with their children, and their neighbors as well. But my friends, it's sad to say in some of these homes today, it is just like being in warfare. There is no safety net, no secure place to rest one's head. Instead, the home is filled with ranting and raving, hatred and strife, and false accusations. Hurtful words, tears, and anger occupy the home. Is this how God wants His people to live, Holy Word?"

"No!" one elderly man shouted out, jumping up from his seat. The church was coming alive; hands clapping, arms waving in the air, and fans moving faster as 'amens' and 'hallelujahs' filled the huge space. Sidney was heating up now as he strutted in front of the crowd.

"Holy Word Holiness," he announced grandly, his arms sweeping to encompass them all.

"As much as it depends on you, live at peace with each other!"

"Amen, Pastor! Amen!"

"Bear with me now, church," he said, loosening his collar.

"The home isn't the only place that warfare is going on."

When his eyes fell upon the place where Yasmin usually sat, he paused, almost having lost his thoughts. *She really isn't here.*

"Lord have mercy," he muttered under his breath and then decided to use the pause theatrically. He didn't want anyone to suspect.

"You know why I got quiet, church? Your place of worship should be peaceful as well. We all know about some of those big ol' churches where all kinds of backstabbing is going on. Y'all know the song by the O'Jays. Right, brothers and sisters?"

Sidney began to sing, *"They smile in your face. All the while they want to take your place."*

The congregation went wild, most old enough to remember the words.

"There are no big I's and little U's in Holy Word Holiness Church," he told the crowd.

"We all are God's children, and He loves every one of us equally, in spite of our shortcomings. And church, that's how we should be toward each other; loving each other, treating one another with respect, honor, and compassion. We shouldn't be... what do the young people say... *haters?*"

"Go on, Pastor Teal!" someone shouted out.

"Amen!"

"We've got to do away with all that backbiting, backstabbing, gossiping, and jealousy in this place of worship. This should be the one place that we can come to get away from all that, and yet it's here too. Y'all know what I'm talking about. Y'all like Sister So-and-So's brand new shoes, but as soon as she can't hear you, y'all talking about how she can't afford them. Y'all see Brother So-and-So's brand new ride, but as soon as he can't hear you, y'all talking about how he's frontin'. But brothers and sisters, we are all God's people, and he expects us to behave as such and live accordingly *every day*, not just on Sunday mornings."

71

Sidney was on a roll as he wiped the sweat from his face. One woman started doing a holy dance right at her seat as she hollered out "hallelujah."

"We should strive to attend to each other's needs, willing to help in any way that we can," Pastor Sidney continued.

"If there be any strife among you today, my brothers and sisters, cast it aside! Cast it aside in our homes, on our jobs, and in our place of worship. We will have peace! Do you hear me, Holy Word!"

"Amen!"

"I hear that, my brother!"

Sidney put a hand to his ear.

"I don't think I heard you, church! I said, we *will* have peace! Do y'all hear me, Holy Word?"

"We hear you!"

"Amen!"

"Praise the Lord, Brother! Preach the word!"

Sidney turned and returned to the podium, sweat drenching his face. The whole church had lit up as if it was the fourth of July. Sidney had done it again. He sat down and basked in the glory.

***

Sidney and Olivia stood with their children in hand at the exit as the members flowed by. For all intents and purposes, they were the perfect family. He shook hands with everyone, remembering most of them by name, complimenting them on their children, or inquiring about their health. Many complimented him on what a fine sermon he preached today, and some new attendees promised to come back next week.

"Hey, Daddy. I'm hungry," Joshua whined, tugging at his father's sleeve.

"Me too, Daddy," Sidney Jr. chimed in. Amia was fast asleep and missed all the cooing and compliments bestowed on her by church members.

CHAPTER SIX

As was the habit on Sundays after church, Sidney and Olivia, with their children, were joined by several other close members for dinner at Etta Mae's Southern Bistro, a local restaurant that, after having been featured on Food Network as one of the best places to eat in America, had become *the* place to be seen. The owner, Etta Mae Williams, also a member of Holy Word, always reserved the largest dining room for Pastor Sidney, his family, and his friends.

While the men were discussing plans for the next seminar scheduled for Tennessee in two weeks, Olivia entertained the deaconesses while trying to keep an eye on the kids. She wasn't thrilled with having to spend time with Johnessa Dixon, Holy Word's answer to *The National Enquirer.* The woman was always up in everyone's business, but Olivia also realized that if anyone knew who Sidney might have been fooling around with, Johnessa would.

"It must be so hard on you having your husbands gone for such long periods of time."

Sister Dixon oozed insincerity as she sipped on her glass of ice water. *Johnessa Dixon is in her mid to late forties, and it shows*, Olivia thought uncharitably, noticing the mounds of foundation the woman caked on to make herself appear younger. Her lipstick was a loud, sparkly color that even the most flamboyant drag queen wouldn't be caught dead in, and the bone straight red hair had to have been India's finest weave. Rumor had it that Gerald Dixon, her husband, had run off with his Asian secretary and that Johnessa was looking for a replacement. Lord knew she had kept Sidney busy in the evenings with her tearful phone calls. The woman would call at all hours of the night, asking for more divine guidance.

Olivia regarded her the same way she would a roach, but her smile was as warm as she could fake it.

"Not really. I've attended some of those seminars, and they can be rather boring. Plus, being away from the children isn't always something I like to do."

"Well," Sister Dixon drawled, her fingernails lightly trailing along the glass.

"At least you don't have to worry about the men getting into trouble since they're far too *busy*. And you know there are some women who attend those kinds of meetings for no good."

The other woman gave Olivia a knowing smirk.

"But it's nice to know that you have such *trust* in Sidney and he in you. Speaking of which, I didn't see Yasmin Lewis in church today."

Olivia cocked her head to the side.

"Really? I didn't notice."

"I don't know how you could *miss* her. She always sits in the same place, right in front of the podium. She's a very nice girl with a great job, but the poor thing is still single."

Sister Dixon sighed dramatically.

"I see that a lot in church. All these beautiful and accomplished sisters, and they're single. I'm sure they all envy you."

As do you, Olivia thought sarcastically.

"I'm sure that all those midnight phone calls to Sidney weren't about scripture either."

Johnessa gave Olivia a lightbulb moment. Suddenly, she looked over at her husband with a sweetly calculating look on her face.

"You know, Sister Dixon, I think I'll accompany Sidney on this trip after all. I was reading through the conference literature, and there are a few seminars, especially for pastors' wives, and I would just *love* to fellowship with them."

***

Sidney tried to keep his mind on the conversation around him, but all he could think about was Yasmin not being in church today. Somehow, he had to get away for a few minutes and call her. She couldn't possibly still be mad at him for having family time. She knew the game, so why was she acting up now? He also needed to know when she was planning to fly out to meet him at the seminar.

"Have all the reservations been made, Sidney?" asked Deacon Ross.

"You know what happened the last time we didn't double-check."

Sidney nodded absently.

"Everything's been taken care of. We'll be leaving bright and early next Monday morning," he assured.

"There's one seminar I've been interested in attending," Sidney started. Then he heard his wife's sudden declaration, and his eyes went wide. He stared at her in disbelief.

What is she talking about? he thought in a panic. *Why does Olivia want to go with me now? Does she know something?* He then spotted Sister Dixon's smirk and wondered just what the woman had said. He had to talk her out of this.

"Honey, isn't this rather sudden? I mean, it's such short notice, and you know how you are about getting someone to babysit."

Just then, Chantel, Ross's wife, piped up.

"I would love to watch the kids for you, Olivia. I mean, if you don't have anyone else in mind."

Olivia's smile this time was open and warm.

"Oh, Chantel, are you sure? It really is such short notice."

Chantel grinned at little Amia, who was playing uneventfully in her booster seat.

"Are you kidding? You know I love the little Rugrats," Chantel said, peering over at the boys.

"And I'll get a chance to practice my mommy skills."

"So, Olivia," Sister Dixon drawled.

"I guess everything is set."

Olivia raised her glass and took a sip of her white wine.

"Yes, Sister Dixon. I think you're right."

***

Dinner was a strained affair for Sidney. Usually, he

78

enjoyed Etta Mae's specialties of the house, especially her twice-baked macaroni and cheese, but for all he knew or cared, he might have been eating dirt.

Talk about throwing a huge monkey wrench into his plans; first Yasmin, and now his wife. No matter how hard he glared at her, she ignored the daggers in his eyes as she chatted with Chantel about the children's schedules. If he didn't know any better, he'd swear both women were out to get him.

How the hell was he going to explain *that* to Yasmin?

***

Instead of sitting inside of Holy Word, staring at a man she shouldn't have and really didn't need, Yasmin was having the time of her life doing all the silly touristy things with Ambrose, from hanging out in Times Square to window shopping on Fifth Avenue. He wanted to see the Guggenheim, so they went there too. The day was a lot cooler with less humidity, as if God approved of Yasmin's choice to play hooky from church and be away from temptation.

Okay, she thought with a smile. Not *too* far away because Ambrose Hunter was definitely tempting. It had been a long time since she went on an actual date with a

79

man where she had fun and where the man was actually interested in her life. Ambrose was unlike Sidney in every way that mattered. He was smart and yet humble. While Sidney enjoyed the finer things in life and wanted everyone to know that he did, Ambrose handled his wealth with tasteful understatement, no diamond-encrusted Rolexes for him.

"A Rolex can't get wet," he told her.

"Or at least most people wouldn't want it to."

Ambrose was adventurous and was knowledgeable about a lot of things. *Granted*, Yasmin thought with a chuckle, *he is more Carlton Banks than Fresh Prince*, but that was okay, even if she didn't quite understand his taste for rock and roll.

Most importantly, the man was a hunk with a capital *H*. She couldn't help but notice the looks she got from not just other sisters, but white women as well. Her chest puffed out with pride since Ambrose seemed unaware of being checked out. He was dressed in Ralph Lauren's casual best: beige khakis, a blue chambray shirt, and matching top-siders. He could have easily been a model.

They strolled around Central Park, watching the horse-drawn carriages and the kids on skateboards. They walked close, and when Ambrose reached out and took her hand, Yasmin thought she'd hit the jackpot.

"I'm glad you said yes to hanging out with me," he said, his voice rich like honey and velvet.

"I had such a good time yesterday, and I really wanted to get to know you a little better."

"Really?" Yasmin squeaked but was happy.

"I thought I wasn't being all that great a guest."

He laughed.

"It's kind of hard to not get overwhelmed by Ronnie and April-Rose. Those two are the life of the party all to themselves."

"Well, it's not like I was doing anything different today. I go to church on Sunday, have dinner with April-Rose, and basically wait for Monday to roll around."

"That sounds like my life too," he said.

"Save the church part. I'll go with friends sometimes, but to be honest, I find the spirit of God looking at the peace of the waves rather than in some building. There's just too much drama in church these days."

"Amen to that," Yasmin agreed, thinking about her own life. Ambrose looked at her.

"So, you're not going to get in my face for not being a good Christian man?"

Yasmin rolled her eyes.

"Considering the kinds of men who claim to be that but are doing everything *but*, you have nothing to worry about."

They continued their walk.

"So, Yasmin Lewis, tell me all about yourself."

Ambrose's sultry voice caressed her name like a kiss, and she shivered deliciously.

"Not much to tell, really."

She shrugged.

"I work for Wheatley & Dunn as a financial consultant, and thankfully, we're in a slow period because when we're not, it's fourteen- to sixteen-hour days."

Ambrose shook his head, grinning.

"I know what those are like. When there's a lucrative real estate client, sometimes I end up sleeping at the office."

Yasmin laughed.

"Now *that's* dedication."

"No, that's *insanity*. The good thing is, it pays very well. So, what else should I know about you?"

"I like to travel, though I have to say I haven't ridden a bike through Denmark."

She smiled at him.

"I prefer a five-star hotel and a nice rental car, and I don't like French food."

"How about Japanese?"

"Love it, but April-Rose refuses to go with me because she thinks I'm going to make her eat raw fish."

"Well then, how about you tell me a great Japanese restaurant, and we can go there for dinner?"

Yasmin was on cloud-nine.

"Okay, Ambrose. I'd love that."

***

"I don't understand what all that was about, Olivia," Sidney started in once they were home and the children had been tucked in. They stood on opposite sides of the bedroom.

"Why the sudden urge to travel with me when you've seldom been interested before?"

Olivia defiantly crossed her arms in front of her chest.

"I could ask why you're suddenly so insistent that I stay *home*, Sidney. Is there something I need to know?"

He sighed, running a hand through his scalp, not wanting to say anything that might set off alarm bells. He was already frustrated with not having seen nor heard from Yasmin all day. He was desperate to call her, but Olivia seemed intent on keeping him occupied. He was beginning to think she knew something about the two of them and wondered exactly what Sister Dixon had told her. Gossiping was a sin. *But so is my affair,* he thought silently.

"This isn't a pleasure trip, honey," he said soothingly.

"It's work. I'll be spending most of the time in a bunch of workshops and seminars, and I won't have any time for you."

"I know all that," she said dismissively.

"In fact, I plan to keep busy by attending a few workshops on my own that are specifically for pastors' wives. It's sad how few of them I actually know, considering that Holy Word has been widely featured."

"Olivia, honey, this is last minute, and I think the hotels are all booked."

"I'd be staying in *your* room, Sidney. I *am* your wife, you know," she replied matter-of-factly. *Great,* Sidney thought despondently. Just great. He tried one more tactic.

"What about the kids? Is it right to just leave them with Chantel? Wouldn't we be imposing? I mean, three kids, Liv? That's a bit much."

Instead of answering right away, his wife looked at him, suspicion in her eyes.

"Why do I get the feeling that you're coming with all these bullshit excuses to keep me from this trip?"

Sidney's mouth gaped open like a fish. Olivia seldom cursed, and he realized how quickly he'd crossed the line.

"Not that it matters, because I *am* going. I'll e-mail my registration and the fee tomorrow morning. I'll also book my flight with you, so if we're finished, I'm going to take a bath. Goodnight."

As Olivia filled the sunken tub with warm water and added her favorite bath salt, she was now more than certain Sidney was cheating on her and was determined to find out who the skank was. Sister Dawson had mentioned Yasmin Lewis, and the way she continued to talk about her raised her alarms. Was she Sidney's hoe?

The girl had an aura about her that attracted men like fruit flies, though to be fair, she never went out of her way to be overly flirtatious, unlike some others in the church who dressed as if they'd just left the Player's Club. Yasmin tended to dress elegantly but tastefully and definitely expensively.

But there were other women as well, and it wouldn't surprise Olivia that Johnessa Dixon was the one actually getting into Sidney's pants.

It was hard to admit that it hurt and that she obviously

wasn't woman enough for Sidney, that she'd given the man fourteen years and three children, and that she had given up her growing career as an interior designer to play the role of the happy housewife like some black June Cleaver. She'd done everything to be the perfect reflection of a preacher's wife. She was actively involved the ministry, from the women's auxiliary groups to working at the women's shelter and hosting all sorts of church events. At one point in time, she'd been very much in love with Sidney Teal, so what the hell had gone wrong?

Perhaps she wasn't as adventurous in bed as he might have liked. Granted, their sex life had waned a little after the kids, but that tended to happen in a lot of marriages. In spite of three children, Olivia still had a nice body and knew how to use it. At one time, Sidney praised her oral skills as she used lips, tongue, and teeth to give him ball-draining orgasms so good that if she had ordered him to kick his mother to the curb, he would have done it.

As she floated in an orange blossom scented haze, Olivia decided that she would not be a victim anymore. As soon as she discovered Sidney's mistress, she would let the entire congregation know. A divorce would devastate the kids, at least in the short term. In the long

86

term, they would learn a valuable lesson about honesty and being faithful.

Olivia valued no ties with Holy Word. Being First Lady wasn't her calling, if truth be known. She would simply take what Sidney would owe her and start all over somewhere he wasn't. She'd always wanted to live out west, and the kids would love California.

***

Sushi Time was a cheesy name, but the food was off the hook. It was one of those mom and pop places that only real foodies and the locals knew about and guarded jealously from the rest of the world. Yasmin had stumbled on the restaurant by accident, and once she'd eaten nearly a hundred dollars' worth of eel and salmon skin rolls, she was hooked.

"It's nothing fancy," she told Ambrose as they entered the restaurant and were quickly greeted by a young Japanese girl with pink hair, wearing some sort of Victorian outfit.

"But the food here is really good."

Ambrose just squeezed her hand.

"I trust you. Besides, I go to a place like this back in L.A."

They ordered the Dinner-for-Two special, which included their choice of sushi and sashimi, but also miso soup, steamed rice, an assortment of pickled vegetables, and spicy chicken gyoza. They were going to order sake, but Ambrose was driving, so they settled on jasmine tea. As they ate, Ambrose regaled her with tales of life as a real estate attorney.

"I don't mind doing the big deals," he said as he sipped on his jasmine tea. Yasmin tried not to think of those perfect lips hugging the rim of the cup against her own.

"But it's when I do the pro bono work, like working with nonprofits to build decent low-income housing and schools. That's when I feel that I'm doing something to give back, especially because you have to fight so many people's perceptions about the kinds of tenants that are going to be living in that housing development."

"I guess they think you're building a project or something," Yasmin said, dipping a piece of tuna sashimi in her soy and wasabi sauce mixture. Ambrose nodded.

"Exactly. The irony is, most of the buildings I've helped with turn out to be extremely nice, and the families who move in do everything to keep them that way. It's the tenants themselves who monitor who goes in or out. Any hint of drugs or other criminal activity, they call the police and have the people evicted."

"So, how did you end up as an attorney?"

He grinned a perfect yet charming grin.

"Simple. I was too nerdy for sports and just so happened to be captain of my high school debate team. Besides, I like the research aspect of the profession."

"The money is not too bad either, right?"

"Not at all, but trust me when I tell you, I earn every bit of it. In fact, as soon as I get back, there will be a mountain of paperwork waiting for me on my desk, and my e-mail inbox will be full. I'll be eating take-out for at least a week while doing those brutal sixteen-hour days."

Yasmin went quiet, not wanting to think about Ambrose returning to L.A. She had never thought about a long-distance relationship. Then again, she hadn't thought of *any* relationship, considering. But now, she didn't want this to end. Ambrose was an amazing man, and she really liked him. Well, they still had a couple of days before that happened. The one thing she did know for certain was Sidney Teal was no longer a factor in any decision she made about her life.

***

"Can I get you something to drink?" Yasmin asked later after the drive back to her condo. She invited Ambrose up, not willing to end the night so soon.

"Just a soda, if you have it," he said. She grabbed a can of Coke and a glass filled with ice. She poured herself a glass of white wine.

"Listen, Yasmin. I had a great time today. I don't know if April-Rose mentioned my last relationship drama, but it's time to move on. I like you, and I get the feeling that you kind of like me a little," he teased.

"Even if you aren't a fan of Sevendust, hang out with me long enough, and I'll get you into a mosh pit before you know it."

She chuckled, rolling her eyes.

"I never said I didn't like them. I'm just an old school R&B girl. Still, I'm always willing to be open-minded. And by the way, I *do* like you."

Ambrose put down the glass of soda and took her slender hand in his.

"Would you like to go out with me tomorrow?"

"Well, duh. There's still Harlem to see, you know?"

His hand felt so warm and right holding hers, as if that was all he wanted to do. For a few moments, there was silence. Then Ambrose brought her hand up to his lips and brushed a kiss against it. Yasmin stifled a gasp, and her body felt all warm and melty like caramel. He winked.

"Then I guess I will see you tomorrow around ten."

***

The moment Ambrose left her doorstep, her cell phone rang.

"Okay, Yaz, spill it!" boomed April-Rose.

"I know you two hit it off."

Yasmin tried to keep her voice steady, but she was as excited as a young girl being asked out by the cutest guy in school.

"Damn, he's everything I want in a man. I really had a great time today, and I didn't think about Sidney once."

April-Rose sent her friend a spiritual high-five.

"That's my girl! You deserve some real happiness, and it's not going to come from being some married man's dessert on the side. I always said you were better than that."

"I know. I know. I guess I was just stuck on stupid."

"I'll say." April-Rose agreed with a chuckle.

"If it makes you feel any better, Pastor Freaky-Deaky was looking in *your* direction at church today, and he was seriously trying hard not to trip 'cause you weren't there.

Me and Ronnie wanted to burst out laughing."

Yasmin stifled her own laugh.

"I'm sure he's going to call soon."

"What are you going to tell him?"

Yasmin didn't hesitate.

"I'm going to tell him it's over."

"And is it, Yaz?" April-Rose asked seriously.

"Ambrose is a decent brother, and I know he'd be good for you, but if you're going to be trifling, then leave him alone."

"No, I'm serious. Today was the first time that a man actually *cared* about what I liked and what I thought. More important, April-Rose, I could spend time with someone like a normal couple."

She heard her friend let out a sigh of relief.

"You don't know how happy I am to hear you finally realize that you're worth more than some man's piece of ass. Leave Sidney Teal to his wife."

CHAPTER SEVEN

Sidney hadn't slept a wink all night. As soon as he was sure his wife was sound asleep, he crept to his office and dialed Yasmin, only to be greeted by her land line voicemail. The same thing happened when he tried her cell phone. For nearly an hour, he sat, wondering what the hell was going on with her. The idea that she'd be with another man was unthinkable, or was it?

If he was perfectly honest with himself, the last time they'd been together, he'd gotten the feeling that Yasmin was just going through the motions. Moreover, maybe it was high time that he let this thing between them just die. Maybe he could salvage his marriage and his family.

He should just give her up, but the minute his mind's eye saw her lush brown curves naked against the crisp white sheets of the elegant hotel they'd been in, Sidney was like a crackhead, jonesing for another hit of the drug known as Yasmin Lewis. He tried her home phone once more. She did not answer.

He woke up early that Monday morning, grabbed his workout bag, kissed Olivia on the cheek, and headed for the gym. Not only did he make it his business to stay in shape for health reasons and for vanity, but a sweat-inducing round of weights and cardio helped him to get his thoughts together.

For what seemed the millionth time, he tried to call Yasmin to no avail. After his workout, he'd try one more time, then drive over to her house to see what was up. He didn't want to consider that she might have been with someone else. That didn't make much sense. When would she have time to meet anyone? She was a workaholic for the most part.

At this time of the morning, the gym was nearly empty, which he was grateful for. He had no interest in making small talk or watching CNN. As he jogged at a steady pace on the treadmill, he thought about Olivia and how the hell he was going to talk her out of attending the conference with him. Nothing came to mind, and he realized the more opposition he gave, the more suspicious she would become.

Even if he wasn't cheating on her, there were times Sidney just wanted to be *away* from the responsibilities of being a husband and a father. It was selfish. He knew. But after the kids came, everything was about *them*. Before, the two of them could have sex anywhere in the damn house they liked, and man, he missed hittin' it with

Olivia. Back then, she had everyone fooled. Everyone thought she was such a proper lady in her expertly tailored clothes, always together hair, and well-manicured nails. But behind closed doors, the woman was a freak with a capital F. She had a body that out-Kimmed Lil' Kim and a nasty mouth that made Lil' Kim sound more like CeCe Winans.

Now, it was playdates, soccer practice, and Dora the Explorer birthday parties. In spite of her being a full-time wife and mother, it just seemed there was no time for them anymore. They both were so busy, and the more Holy Word grew, the busier he was. Sometimes, he wondered if it was all too much. That was why he needed the breathing room, especially now when he felt his life was reaching a crossroads.

***

Yasmin rose and stretched. Her body was all tingly just thinking about seeing Ambrose again. The day was bright and sunny, and once more, the humidity was dropping to more normal levels. It was going to be a wonderful day. She could feel it.

She checked her voicemail and shook her head at Sidney's voice on the phone asking her to call him. Sooner or later, he'd get the message that she was done.

In fact, she decided before bed last night to buy a new cell phone—maybe the new HTC one with the cute little charm that was actually a Bluetooth signal to let her know she had a call. She would get a new number as well. Unfortunately, he knew where she lived, which meant she'd have to deal with him one more time to tell him it was over.

As she showered, she thought about Ambrose. He lived on the West Coast. Did it even make sense to start something with him? Who knew when he'd be out this way again? Not to mention, there were plenty of single women who'd love to get their hands on a successful, somewhat proper brother. She decided right then, even if they just remained friends, her days as Sidney Teal's mistress were over for good. Even if she had to find another church, she'd never allow herself to get caught up in that kind of drama ever again. It was nothing short of the Lord's work that the two of them hadn't gotten caught.

After drying off and slathering her skin with a homemade body soufflé, she dressed in casual Cookie Johnson jeans, a flowing Georgette tunic top, and Papilio sandals. It was a cute yet kind of Boho look, especially when she tied a flowing print scarf like a headband

96

around her head and added large silver hoops to her ears.

Her doorbell rang, and her heart began skipping like a child in a cartoon show. With a huge shit-eating grin, Yasmin practically skipped to her front door, eyes shining and her entire body vibrating with excitement. It didn't even matter that Ambrose was one hour early. They could just hang out here while she made coffee and warmed up some banana nut bread.

She threw open the door with a "hi, Ambrose" poised on her lips. She was shocked and dismayed to Sidney standing in the doorway of her apartment.

"What are *you* doing here?"

He looked at her.

"I tried to call you numerous times."

"I know," Yasmin replied coldly. "I didn't answer. It's over."

He stood with his arms folded.

"Can I at least come in?"

Yasmin stepped aside as Sidney entered her apartment. She didn't offer him coffee or ask him to sit, since she planned to have him long gone before Ambrose came to pick her up.

"There's nothing you can say that will change my mind, Pastor Teal. It's over, and if I had any sense, it

97

should never have started."

"So, when did this all happen?" he asked coldly. "Is there someone else? Someone else who kept you away from church yesterday?"

"Not that it's any of your business, but yes. And even if there wasn't, I finally woke up and smelled the coffee. I get nothing out of this situation. You'll never leave your wife and kids, and I'll just be lonely and bitter, waiting for you to have free time."

She shook her head bitterly.

"I'd rather be single and alone because I'd at least have my self-respect."

"You promised to be mine, Yasmin, all mine and no one else's," Sidney stated quietly.

"I was young, stupid, and naïve back then, Sidney. I would have promised you the moon. Frankly, I like being with a man with no baggage."

Sidney wasn't listening to her at all.

"When the hell where you going to drop this on me, Yasmin? Were you scared to tell me the truth? And I know it's not easy for you, but haven't I been good to you?"

Hands on her hips, she gave him a pitying look.

"Excuse me if I want more than the little you can

squeeze out here and there. You seem to think all those expensive little trinkets must mean something, as if I'm some sort of gold-digger."

Yasmin turned around and presented Sidney with a shoebox. When he opened it, his eyes went wide, looking as if she'd slapped him.

"That's everything you've given me, Sidney. I never wore any of it, because it wasn't right. No matter how much you spent, it made me feel cheap. Give it to Olivia if you want."

He tried to approach her, but she sidestepped him.

"Is this because I cancelled our last date?"

Yasmin just shook her head, unbelieving. How the hell could she have ever loved this man? He had the gall to act like he owned her or something. A date? What she was going to have today with Ambrose was *a date*. What she had with Sidney Teal was him wanting to have his cake and eating it too. Yasmin took a deep breath and let all the emotions she had carried for so long overflow like a rain-swollen river.

"What part of 'it's over' do you not seem to understand, Sidney?"

Yasmin rounded on him, unleashing the full force of her rage.

"I am so damn tired of being at your beck and call like some stupid little puppet. I've wasted so much time waiting for you to fit me into your life. I've been blind to other men—*single* men—because I thought I wanted to be with you. It took some serious soul searching to finally realize how stupid I've been. This whole thing has always been about *you*, not *me*."

"Yasmin, baby, I'm sorry that I haven't spent as much time with you as I should have," he started, once again trying to embrace her, but he paused at her unapproachable stance.

"I've tried to give you all the time that I can, but I never lied to you about how this was going to have to be, and you never complained before."

"That's because when I did complain, *you* didn't give a fuck," she retorted. He flinched.

"I have way too much going for me to get all hung up on a man that I will never have. And you know something, Sidney? It's nice to be able to go out in public without having to worry that someone from Holy Word will see us together. It's nice to be with someone who treats me with respect—two things you could *never* do."

Sidney was about to say something else, but Yasmin held up her hand.

"Save it, Pastor Teal, for someone who cares. We're done, so now you can leave. I've got to finish getting ready for my *date*."

She turned and headed for the kitchen to make coffee. Over her shoulder, she tossed in a final parting shot.

"There's the door. I suggest you use it."

***

Across town, another couple was breaking up—one that was still legally married.

Sylvester Goodings was on his knees, begging for Dana, his wife of several years, to look at him instead of randomly tossing all of her clothes into a large suitcase.

"Dana, baby, please."

Dana Goodings whipped her silky locs in his direction, the soul-deep pain of betrayal on her face.

"Please *what*? You *promised* me! You *promised* God to honor and cherish me! You *knew* what I went through with my mother having to live with this shit for years from my no-good daddy, and you went right on ahead and did it anyway. I just hope the bitch had a million-dollar pussy because at least you'd have something to show for it!"

"Baby, baby, I know I was wrong, but I swear it didn't mean anything," he pleaded.

"I guess it doesn't mean anything that I might have some kind of disease, Sylvester! What if the bitch is *pregnant*? Did you even stop to think about that? That skanky ho you slept with probably has herpes or AIDS or something, and you didn't even care that you might have brought that shit home!" Dana wheeled back and continued packing. When her husband tried to touch her, she drew back, shaking with rage.

"Don't touch me!" she yelled.

"You're just like my trifling ass daddy. He told my mama the same bullshit over and over again, that it was only *one time,* that he'll never do it again, and my mama believed him 'cause she wanted us to have a daddy. She believed the man right up to the day she died, and he wasn't even in there in the hospital room, because he was with some other bitch! Well, I ain't my mama, and I ain't going down like that!"

There was nothing Sylvester could do—at least for now. He knew it was a risk coming clean about his indiscretion, and he knew there was a good chance that Dana would be angry and hurt.

In retrospect, he should have known how she felt about infidelity. They'd talked about the subject while they were still dating, and even then, Dana had strong opinions about anyone—man or woman—who cheated on a spouse. Then again, she'd lived with it until age eighteen, and seeing what it had done to her mother had made her unforgiving on this one failing. She told him once, "A real man doesn't think with his dick." He'd laughed and agreed wholeheartedly.

Sylvester had friends who dealt with all sorts of baby mama drama because they couldn't or wouldn't control their manhood. He thought himself better than that. He'd been wrong.

He tried one more time.

"Dana, please. I am so sorry, and I swear to God that I will *never* hurt you like this again. Give me another chance. Give *us* another chance."

This time, there were tears in her eyes.

"I'm sorry, Sylvester, but I can't. There is no us anymore."

She closed up the overstuffed suitcase.

"When you dance to the music, you've got to pay the piper."

Sylvester sat in the empty and silent house, drinking himself into oblivion. Everything reminded him of Dana—from the African masks adorning the walls, to the pink satin throw pillows that said DIVA. Her scent, a mixture of roses, coconut, and sandalwood, was everywhere. Her laughter, the way she walked, that way she raised her eyebrows, and her afterimage was all around him.

He had the Chi-Lites on repeat. "Oh Girl" reminded him of what a moment's pleasure had cost him. Where would he find another strong and beautiful black woman like Dana? She'd always had his back. Pastor Sidney warned him that she might react this way and that he needed to be ready for it, but God, it was hard; so hard.

Sylvester sobbed quietly. His heart shattered into a million pieces. He tried to call her cell phone, but every call just went to voicemail.

In a drunken haze, he got into their Chrysler 300 and went out to find his wife. His head spun, and everything was a blur. He loved Dana so much. She was his entire world, and no other woman would ever do. He prayed that if God were to ever give him another chance, he'd be a far better man, and she'd have no cause to leave him.

He sped down the street, paying no attention to how fast he was going. The next thing he heard was the screeching of brakes and a bright flash of light. Then everything went blank.

CHAPTER EIGHT

Sidney didn't remember most of the drive home. He was simply numb. Yasmin was out of his life for good. They'd had a couple of arguments like this in the past about him making more time for her and about her feeling unloved, but he'd usually been able to soothe her feelings, and the make-up sex was always amazing.

If he was honest with himself, he knew this day was coming, and he should have prepared better for it. More importantly, it was time to let her go. Man cannot serve two masters, and here he was trying to serve two women. There really was no reason now to keep Olivia from travelling with him to the conference.

Still, it hurt far more than he'd thought it would. Despite what Yasmin thought, he'd come to care a great deal about her. She'd been like a safe haven in the storm of his life. Unlike so many other women out there, she could take care of herself. He would miss that warm smile and the feel of her perfect lips against his own.

As he stood in the shower, the hot water ran down his back. He should have known better. He was stupid for getting his heart involved or for trying to make her be faithful to him. What right did he have to ask that of her?

As he was lying in his satin pajamas, idly flicking channels on the flat screen television, his thoughts drifted back to the last conversation they'd had. Had there been anything he could have said that would have changed her mind? Maybe he could have promised to spend more time with her, no matter how hard keeping such a promise would be, especially now with Olivia being more suspicious. He thought of the box of gifts Yasmin had shoved in his face. Most of them were still wrapped as if she took them and then put them away. It was ironic that she wasn't a gold digger. He could think of a lot of women who'd floss those kinds of expensive gifts without a second thought.

He ran a hand across his aching forehead. It was stupid for him to be so hung up on a woman who could never be his. He should be grateful that all the lies were finally over and that he didn't get caught. He should be thinking of ways to strengthen his marriage. Yasmin Lewis had never been *his* woman, and it was time for him to get it together, but that was easier said than done. Sidney couldn't help wondering who the new man in her life was.

***

Yasmin promised herself that she would remember

this day for the rest of her life. It was like she'd been just existing and not living. She'd lived in New York for so long that her southern drawl was a distant memory, but she'd never really seen it through someone else's eyes. Then again, how many places had Sidney taken her to? Harlem was the black mecca, and she'd never once walked its historic streets until Ambrose.

They strolled down Odell Clark Place, home of Abyssinian Baptist Church where Adam Clayton Powell once preached.

"Wow, this church is huge!" exclaimed Yasmin.

"But I don't feel like I'd ever be lost."

Ambrose nodded.

"So many great things happened here. A lot of people think Civil Rights just happened down South."

Next, they wandered down Hamilton Heights, a tree-lined avenue that had been a part of the Harlem Renaissance. The elegant stone row houses were still in mint condition. They hit Strivers' Row next, so named because poorer Harlemites thought those who lived there were "striving" to become well-to-do.

"I read these houses date back to around the 1890's," Ambrose said as he and Yasmin took pictures of the gorgeous neo-Italian homes.

"Think of all the black families who lived here and made it despite all the racism around them."

Yasmin agreed.

"Yeah, but let some folks tell it, we were always poor, down, and out. We never had anything like black doctors and lawyers."

Ambrose chuckled.

"Don't you know that we didn't have any black lawyers until Clare Huxtable?"

They both cracked up at that.

Yasmin was so glad she'd worn comfortable walking shoes because she wanted to see everything, and Ambrose was more than willing to go along. It was obvious he was into black history, and seeing it for himself just made it more real. His passion was infectious, and she told him so.

As they headed toward Sugar Hill, Yasmin said to him, "Maybe you should have been a history teacher instead of an attorney. You really get into this stuff."

"I really do, Yasmin," he said softly.

"It makes me humble and thankful for all those who paved the path for me. You know?"

Sugar Hill had once been the home of W.E.B. DuBois and Thurgood Marshall, while not too far away, Langston

Hughes and Zora Neale Hurston wrote, and Duke Ellington and Count Basie played.

They wandered down Marcus Garvey Avenue and Malcolm X Boulevard. They posed in front of the world famous Apollo Theater, gazing at all the classic posters from the heady days of soul music. There were plenty of places to eat and to shop. Ambrose discovered Hue-Man Bookstore, and Yasmin watched with amusement as he racked up nearly $200 worth of books. He had the chance to return the favor when she practically ran him over trying to get inside of Carol's Daughter, the famous bath and body place. She went buck wild and didn't seem to care if she was maxing out her American Express card.

"At least I'll *smell* good and have soft skin," she quipped.

"And I notice you bought some stuff from her men's line."

"Guilty as charged."

***

By the time Ambrose pulled up to her apartment, Yasmin was happily tired, full to bursting from the delicious dinner they'd had, and a little tipsy from the wine tasting at The Winery, which specialized in local wines. She'd made a mental note to herself to shop there

110

from now on whenever she planned to entertain. The young sales clerk, a bantu-knotted black man whose family owned a winery in California's wine country, had been a wonderful resource.

She'd even gotten hip to King's X, a hard rock trio which featured a black lead singer and bass player named Doug Pinnick. If anything could be said of Ambrose Hunter, it was that he was helping her slowly expand her horizons.

"You know, Ambrose," she said, loving the way his name tasted on her lips.

"Until I met you, it just seemed like I've been stuck in this little box or something. I don't know. It's like my life was so boring and routine. I mean, I traveled here and there, but I haven't done the stuff *you* do. You seriously make me want to be more adventurous."

He helped her take her packages up to her apartment and held them as she dug out her keys.

"Actually, it's you I should be thanking, Yasmin. I was planning to stay home and dwell on my heartbreak, but Ronnie convinced me I needed a break, and he was so right."

He carefully put the bags on the dining room table and took her hand.

"I wouldn't have met you, and that would have been a shame."

When his lips met hers, Yasmin swore she heard angels. It was a soft kiss, no tongues or teeth, and it was a kiss that expected nothing in return. It was a kiss from a man who respected a woman, but also one from a man who knew how to kiss. A part of her wanted more and wanted to take him into her bedroom and finally erase all traces of Sidney Teal from her body and mind. A bigger and wiser part that had grown over the past few days realized that she didn't need to do that. Instead, when their lips parted, she gave him a quick peck on the cheek.

"How about dinner here tomorrow?" she asked shyly. He smiled, and the room just seemed to brighten.

"I'll be here."

When Ambrose left and she closed the door softly behind her, Yasmin Lewis did a happy dance as if she'd been set free from prison.

"Thank you, Lord," she prayed fervently.

"Thank you for showing me the *right* way."

CHAPTER NINE

Olivia was in the kitchen with Sidney's mother and Sister Mary Jordan, who lived couple of homes down in their gated community. Sister Jordan had become a good friend to Olivia as well as a good neighbor. All three women were busy preparing Sunday's dinner. Delicious smells from the oven circulated throughout the kitchen as Mother Teal fixed a huge pot of her heavenly collard greens with ham hocks and bacon, baked chicken with a mouth-watering cornbread dressing, and Olivia's special macaroni and cheese. For dessert, there would be a sweet potato pie and peach cobbler.

At age seventy, Clara Teal was still a very striking and forceful presence. She had elegant salt and pepper hair, which made her deep brown skin stand out even more. Clara wore her seventy years far better than some women who were ten years her junior. She adored her oldest son, almost to the point of worship, but she did not love Olivia any less. In fact, Mother Teal and Olivia got along very well. She told everyone that Olivia was the daughter she never had, and Olivia shared her sentiments. She'd always felt that she could confide in Mother Teal when it came to good solid advice without fear of being judged. Olivia loved her own mother just as much, but

Kathleen Smith had never really been a demonstrative woman.

And like all grandmothers, Mother Teal spoiled her grandkids outrageously, especially little Amia who always knew when "grammy" was in town.

Olivia was lost in thought, stirring the pot of collards when Mother Teal's warm voice nudged her thoughts.

"What's going on in that head of yours, Livvy?" Mother Teal questioned kindly.

"You haven't been yourself since I got here. Is everything alright?"

Olivia didn't want to air her business in front of Sister Jordan, but she also knew the other woman would keep what she heard to herself until the grave.

"I'm fine, Mother Teal. I'm fine," Olivia replied quietly.

"I haven't been sleeping much lately."

Mother Teal's brown eyes sparkled merrily.

"Child, are you pregnant?"

She winked, teasing Olivia.

"Heavens no! Three children are more than enough for me!"

"So I gather you and my son are finished with all that now?"

The younger woman nodded.

"We have three beautiful and smart children, and that's more than anyone could ask."

Mother Teal pursed her lips.

"Well, I know Sidney did mention the idea of having another child, but that's all it was—*a thought*."

Olivia tried not to grit her teeth. Leave it to Sidney to decide what she could do with her body. She said archly, "As far as I'm concerned, we are definitely done with having any more kids. If it was left up to your son, we'd look like the black version that old show *Eight Is Enough*."

Mother Teal patted her shoulder.

"It's not my business, but child, you both is too young to stop so soon."

Olivia just smiled, even though she really wanted to tell her mother-in-law that it wasn't her business at all. Instead, she said, "The kids are growing up, and I'd like to do something else with my life besides being a wife and a mother. You know I had a great interior design business when I married Sidney. A lot of women are working moms these days."

"I know that, honey, but children are a blessing from God."

"I understand that, Mother Teal, but I don't think He meant for me to populate the whole world."

She chuckled dryly. Olivia sighed. They'd had this conversation many times before. The only thing that irritated her about Mother Teal was the fact she thought Sidney walked on water. Why wasn't she on her youngest son, Franklin's, back about finally settling down and giving her some damn grandkids? That man spent more time being broke and running to Sidney or his mother whenever he needed money for some high-faulting scheme. Then again, the way Franklin Teal went through women, Mother Teal might have a whole bunch of grandkids and not even know it.

Olivia hated to admit that, for a long time, she had been a lot like her mother-in-law. Early on in their marriage, she deferred to him in all things as she once thought a good Christian wife should. Back then, he made all the decisions, and she never questioned him on any of them. After some years, Olivia decided that just wasn't working.

"Well, if it's not kids, what *is* bothering you? Don't you dare go beating around the bush. I know you as if you were my own," Mother Teal admonished as she checked on the baked chicken in the oven.

Olivia debated on telling her mother in-law what was really bothering her. How could she tell her mother-in-law about the suspicions she had concerning her son's fidelity? She took a deep breath and went for it.

"How do you know if your husband is… well… *cheating* on you?" she asked quickly. The older woman's face went ashen as she stared at her daughter-in-law as if she'd sprouted three heads. Even Sister Jordan had gone silent from the spiritual song she was humming.

"Chile, where in the world did you come up with such nonsense?" Mother Teal demanded.

"You can't possibly think my Sidney is cheating on you."

Mother Teal looked quite upset. The cat was now out of the proverbial bag, but she tried to smooth things over.

"I didn't say he *was*. I just want to know what the signs are. Married women ask this question all the time, right?"

Mother Teal took a seat at the walnut-topped breakfast nook, took a cotton handkerchief out of her apron pocket, and began wiping her face.

"Well, I really don't know what to say, Livvy. Why would you ask something like that unless you think he *is* cheating on you?"

She gazed hard at Olivia.

"My Sidney would *never* do such a thing to you and those children. That man loves y'all dearly with every breath he takes," she replied with certainty in her voice. Olivia sat down beside her.

"I just asked you how a woman would know *if* her husband was cheating on her. I don't think Sidney is, but sometimes things begin happening in a marriage, things start changing, and well, it makes it different."

She knew she sounded lame to her ears, and that she was lying through her perfect teeth about believing Sidney was being faithful to her, but she really needed to know.

"I'll answer that question for you, Olivia."

Sister Jordan dusted the flour from her hands, took a glass of water from the countertop, and sat in the empty chair beside her friend.

"Look the man directly in his eyes and ask him straight out. The eyes never lie," she said. Mother Teal shot the other woman an accusing look and retorted, "If the woman is a good wife and mother, she wouldn't *need* to ask that question."

But Sister Jordan wasn't the kind of woman to back down.

"A woman could be June Cleaver in the kitchen and Lil' Kim in the bedroom, and a man will still cheat if he has the chance. That's just how they are."

She looked straight at Olivia.

"Just look at me and Bill. We've been married almost twenty-five years, and I'll be the first to tell you that along the way, there were some question marks here or there, but I never dwelled on it. He took care of me and the kids, brought home the bacon, and took care of business. He treated me well then and still does. Whatever might have or didn't happen along the way didn't amount to a hill of beans, because I have him, and *they* don't."

Olivia couldn't believe what she was hearing. She thought she knew her friend well.

"You're saying as long as the man is taking care of his business at home, the wife should just let sleeping dogs lie?"

Sister Jordan smiled thinly.

"As long as he's not puttin' it all out in the street and embarrassing you, just smile and be the good little wifey. Believe me, once they see what real lovin' is, they'll come back home."

Even Mother Teal was troubled by Sister Jordan's answer.

"If you have a good man, and a God-fearing man at that, you won't have to worry about no mess like cheating."

Sister Jordan was not willing to give up her point.

"I don't care how good they are. Given the opportunity, a man will cheat. It's in their nature."

Olivia could see a storm brewing between the two women. This was obviously a topic which touched some nerves.

"Okay, you two."

Olivia held her hands up like a mother separating a pair of squabbling kids.

"No one has answered the question. How do you *know* if a man is cheating on you? I mean, what are the signs?"

Both women went quiet, then Mother Teal cleared her throat.

"I'd say very little communication."

"Paying no attention to you," Sister Jordan added.

"Dressing or acting differently than he usually does."

"Coming home and going straight to bed," answered Mother Teal.

"Or getting up earlier than usual."

"Less sex," said Sister Jordan.

"Or no sex."

She smirked. That did it. Mother Teal slammed her hand down on the table.

"Let me tell both of you young'uns something. I've been around longer than both of you, and I think I know a little something about life."

She glared at Sister Jordan.

"I agree, some men will cheat, and for that matter, some *women* will as well. But if you have a good solid marriage and it's worth fighting for, you shouldn't let nothin' or nobody tear it down. D'you hear?"

Olivia nodded quietly. Her mind was still not at ease, and in spite of her mother-in-law's best intentions, there were more questions than answers. The older woman smiled gently at her.

"Now, don't you let no notion come into that head that your husband is doing anything other than serving his God and being dutiful to his calling. I raised Sidney David Teal right, and he knows I don't play."

Mother Teal rose gracefully.

"Now let's finish up this here cookin'. We're gonna have us some hungry menfolk to feed tomorrow."

CHAPTER TEN

Sidney and Ross sat in the church office, still reeling over Brother Goodings' tragic accident. The doctors said it was a miracle the young man was still alive since he'd wrapped the car around a lamp post. In his lucid moments, the poor man was asking for Dana, his wife, but it was as if she'd dropped off the face of the earth. He'd told Sidney he confessed to cheating, and she'd left him. Sidney could only imagine what her reaction would be when she found out what had happened.

His own mind was uneasy. Two weeks had gone by since Yasmin dumped him. He had no right to feel that way, considering they never really had a *relationship*. He had no right to feel like she had betrayed him, and yet that's precisely what he did feel. He didn't know what to do about that, nor did he know what to do about his wife. Should he tell her? Thinking of poor Sylvester hooked up to an IV machine and his jaw wired shut, didn't seem like a good thing. Then again, Olivia wasn't the melodramatic type. She'd just coldly divorce him, take half of everything, *and* she'd take the kids.

That last morning when he went to Yasmin's apartment, he'd never seen her so alive, so happy, and so full of life. She was like a totally new person. It was as if

123

the last three years hadn't happened. She had no right to look so good when he felt so bad. In a strange way, he realized he'd come to love her.

"Maybe it wasn't worth it," Sidney said, twiddling his fingers in front of him. Ross looked at his friend's pensive expression.

"You mean Sylvester telling his wife about cheating on her?"

Sidney nodded slowly.

"He promised me he was done and that he was going to do everything he could to make things right. Maybe if he kept that promise, there wouldn't have been a need to tell her anything."

Ross shrugged.

"They say confession *is* good for the soul. Besides, you know the saying about what happens in the dark coming to light. What would happen if the other woman came along and decided to start some mess?"

"Like if she's pregnant?"

"Yeah. Just that alone can cause a whole lot of drama."

Sidney sighed.

"I counseled him on saving his marriage, but sometimes I just don't know, Ross. I know what scripture says, but are we men really meant to be with one woman? I see so much of this stuff happening, and sometimes I just wonder."

Ross was a little shocked by his friend's comment. Sidney Teal was a God-fearing man. Surely, someone like him should have no doubts as to what marriage meant.

"The reason it's happening is because people want everything with no consequences," Ross began.

"Marriage is hard work, but few folks see it that way. When things get difficult, they go running off to someone else or start doing drugs or whatever. Me and Chantel are having a hell of a time over this baby business, but we both want to be parents. It's hard because my mama has never liked Chantel in the first place, and she thinks my wife really doesn't want kids but is scared to lose me. Man, you don't know all the drama going on when my mom starts up, but we are in this thing for the long haul."

Sidney laughed, having a similar experience with his own mother who wanted more grandkids.

"God knows I love Olivia, but sometimes I don't feel like I'm *in love* with her. It's like she's someone I don't recognize anymore."

Ross raised a questioning eyebrow. He didn't want to

125

know, but he also knew Sidney would tell him anything.

"You're not cheating on her, are you?"

The look on the other man's face and his silence said it all.

"Man, are you serious? What on earth made you step out on her?"

Ross was shocked at the confession, but he needed to understand his friend and perhaps set him straight.

"She's a wonderful woman and still beautiful. You don't hear what some of the younger brothers in the church say about her, but they think you're a lucky man. Plus, she's given you three beautiful kids."

Sidney wrung his hands.

"I know all that. I have a great life, and yet something was missing at home. No, things just started changing when Olivia had Amia. Suddenly, it was all about the children. She stopped wanting to make love because she was afraid the boys would hear us. Now she's talking about restarting her interior design business. I just felt like I was losing ground, and I was weak."

Ross said nothing as Sidney's voice broke. Something inside of him seemed shattered or broken.

"Worse is that the woman I was seeing just dumped me out of the blue. I know I don't have the right to be mad, but I think I was falling in love with her."

"That's not love my, man. You're infatuated."

When Sidney looked up, he saw an understanding wisdom in Ross's eyes.

"You wanted a woman who reminded you of what your wife used to be and of what you can't have. You're mad because *she* dumped *you.* Normally, it's the other way around."

Sidney hated to admit the truth of Ross's last statement. It was a blow to his ego. Not only had Yasmin dumped him, but she had another man waiting in the wings. Oddly enough, Beyoncé's song "Irreplaceable" came to mind. He smiled ironically. She'd even packed up a box of stuff he'd given her.

"Look, Sidney. I'm not going to get all off in your business any more than I already have, but everything that has happened is a huge ass neon sign from God. Brother Goodings almost lost his life, but he for damn sure has lost his wife. I really hate to see us brothers messing over good black women this way. No wonder more of them are headed for the vanilla express. Not to mention, the Lord has blessed you a thousand-fold. Your ministry is thriving. You're well-known around the country, and you're living a life most people can't even dream of. More importantly, through all your struggles to get to this point, Olivia has been right by your side. Don't you think she deserves a lot more than a husband who doesn't seem to appreciate her?"

From anyone else, Sidney would have made excuses, but Ross was too smart and too much of a best friend to be fooled. The man was right about it all, and yet, in a small place within his heart, Yasmin Lewis still lived.

"So, should I be like Sylvester and come clean?"

Ross folded his arms over his chest.

"That's up to you to decide, my man."

He stood up.

"I'm going to go visit Sylvester. I think he could use some friends and some serious prayer."

Sidney agreed, knowing that prayer definitely could change things. Hopefully, even him.

***

Sylvester had never hurt so much, but it wasn't the injuries to his ribs, his jaw, his skull, and his left foot. His heart and soul hurt, and unlike his body, he believed the only way those would heal was for Dana to come back, even if she never forgave him, but just to have her there to see her face.

For the billionth time, he cursed himself for being so stupid. Dana was a good woman. She'd always had his back, and she was everything any man could have wanted. No, that wasn't true. She *was* everything, and like a greedy child, he wanted more.

Some of his buddies were no help since most of them thought that cheating on their wives or girlfriends was a guy's prerogative. They used to laugh at him and call him whipped because he tried his best to honor his vows. Those same buddies weren't even by his bedside, not that he'd want them around. Listening to them was what got him in this mess in the first place.

No, what got him into trouble was his own selfishness. A grown man thinks with his head, and it was not the one between his legs. Thinking back to the few times he spent with Terri, he couldn't forget her, even though he wanted to. It had been just empty and meaningless sex, a way to get his rocks off. He didn't even know *why* he had sex with her in the first place. Dana fulfilled all his needs, even in the bedroom.

A part of him just didn't want to go on living without his wife, but living was a suitable punishment. Every lonely day and even lonelier night would remind him of what he'd so foolishly thrown away. It would serve him

129

right if one day Dana walked down the street with another man, wearing another man's ring.

***

Dana Goodings stood five feet ten and was built like a brick house. She was proud of her flawless dark skin, the shade of perfect sable. She wore her hair in a big healthy afro, having almost lost most of it to years of chemical upon chemical damaging it. The day she went natural was the best day of her life. Sylvester used to run his fingers through it and help her braid it into four sections at night. The memory of his smile and his tenderness hurt like hell.

She came to the hospital after having spent hours debating with herself whether or not to see him one last time. It was hard to forget how much she loved him and how proud of him she'd been when he graduated from SUNY with a degree in Information Technology. She remembered her friends warning her about Tyler Perry-ing herself by marrying down instead of up, as most of them had done. But there had been something about Sylvester that said he would never be content managing a McDonald's, which was where they met, especially when he showed her how he'd modified his laptop to respond to his voice. It was a geeky thing, but being into technology herself, it had been the way to her heart.

He'd been so different from most of the black men she'd dealt with, the ones with their fake swagger and their disrespect toward black women. It was an attitude Dana did not put up with, unlike her mother who had for years. Sylvester had been almost shy when he first approached her. He was like one of those medieval knights, all chivalrous and honorable. They didn't even kiss until the third date, and though neither had a religious issue with having sex before marriage, they just wanted to wait because they knew it would be special.

When Sylvester was hired by Goldman Sachs' IT department, Dana just couldn't help bragging to the same girlfriends who downed her for "slumming."

The two of them had become the new face of young successful Black America. Their home straddled the glorious past of Africa with art and artifacts from the motherland, the future with all the latest technological gadgets two high-salaries could ever afford, and an autographed and framed picture of President Barack Obama.

Granted, those five years hadn't been all wine and roses, and like so many young couples, they'd had their share of arguments and disagreements, but there had never been the slightest doubt the love was strong. It had

131

been Sylvester's plea that no matter what went down between them during the day, they should never go to bed angry. They never did. There were times both spent all night handling their issues, listening, and trying to understand. Dana knew the two of them were slowly but surely building the perfect marriage.

Her heels clicked against the scuffed and worn linoleum, heart racing inside of her chest. What would she find when she opened the door to his room?

***

"Hey, man, no more ribs for you for a long time," Sidney teased Brother Goodings who managed a weak chuckle. The nurse said the anesthesia had worn off and that he could receive visitors.

Ross laughed too and said, "Unless they put 'em in a blender first."

The two men looked down at their friend and church member. They had expected far worse and silently thanked the Lord that it wasn't, though Sylvester Goodings wasn't going to be running any marathons anytime soon.

Sidney felt especially bad because he'd been the one to counsel Sylvester into telling Dana the truth, and look what happened. As if he could read the other man's thoughts, Sylvester's eyes met his.

No, you were right, Pastor, his eyes seemed to be saying to him. *I needed to confess, and even though this happened, my soul feels lighter. I may have lost Dana, but I plan to do everything I can to get her back.*

The unspoken words almost brought tears to Sidney's eyes. Then the door opened, and in walked Dana, her beautiful brown, amber eyes wide. Sidney and Ross quickly moved to leave to give the two of them some privacy, but Dana shook her head.

"I won't be here long," she said quietly.

"I wanted to see him. I'm not unfeeling, you know?"

Then she looked at her husband as she slowly loosened the platinum and fair-trade diamond band around her finger. She took it off and gently laid it on his chest.

"I can't wear this anymore, because it doesn't mean anything."

She sniffled.

"You know I didn't even like diamonds because of the slave labor used to get them, but you went out of your way to find ones that weren't bought with blood. I wore it because you showed me love and that I mattered. Now, I

133

just feel empty. I don't even feel hate, because that would at least be some kind of emotion. I feel *nothing*."

Tears welled up in Sylvester's eyes, the ring on his chest pressing into him like a ton of bricks. He could not speak and could not beg. He was losing her, and there wasn't a damn thing he could do about it now. How much worse could his life possibly get?

The answer to *that* question barged into the hospital room in a shower of expensive perfume and designer clothes. Dana insolently looked into the face of the woman who'd caused so much misery and just felt *nothing*. Even if she wanted to go all Jerry Springer on the bitch's ass, she just didn't care enough to do so. Meanwhile, Sidney and Ross stared at each other, wondering whether they were soon going to find themselves in the middle of a serious beat-down.

The other woman ran to Sylvester's side.

"Oh, baby, I just heard! I came over as soon as I could before heading to the airport. I'm sorry I can't stay long, but I'm on my way to Milan for a show, and I hear the Valentino people are insane!"

She tried to place a kiss on his lips, but Sylvester quickly turned his head away. Shocked, she looked at him, then the ring on his chest, then at the woman behind her. Concern and worry instantly gave way to rage.

"Oh h-to-the-e-to-the-double-l no! You are *not* going to tell me you're married!"

Dana rolled her eyes, feeling a bit sorry for her rival.

"I guess he forgot to mention *that* little detail, and I guess you never suspected."

The tension was so thick you could cut it with a knife. Both women stood staring at each other, having completely forgotten the reason they were here. Terri just shook her head.

"Yeah, I know. I should have paid attention to the signs, but I'm always busy on a shoot somewhere, so I figured if I saw Sylvester every so often, that was cool. I don't have the time to be tied down."

"So tell me, Terri," Dana said the other woman's name like a cuss word.

"When was the last time you saw *Sylvester*?"

"Oh, about a month or so ago. We had dinner in the city and then went back to my apartment in Tribeca."

Dana was absolutely numb. She could not even breathe.

A *month* ago, she and Sylvester had celebrated their seventh wedding anniversary. A *month* ago, they'd

135

planned a romantic getaway to the Hamptons. A *month* ago, he was working late in the IT department, trying to circumvent that virus that had businesses worldwide scrambling. And a *month* ago, he was sticking his dick into some Tyra Banks wannabe while she was running around with a simple ass smile on her face and bragging to her friends about how good he was to her. Worse still was that he'd told the other woman he was *single*.

It was all just too much. Dana didn't say another word. She just turned around and walked out of his room and out of his life, permanently.

***

Sidney felt the touch of the Lord on his shoulder, and he knew what he had to do, or at least try to. He dashed out of Sylvester's hospital room and managed to catch Dana stepping into the elevator. As if through divine intervention, they were the only two people inside.

"Don't even start with me, Pastor Teal. I don't want a sermon about forgiveness or any of that bullshit, 'cause I'm not trying to hear it," Dana spat. She began shaking.

"His other woman just walks right on in, and I'm standing there like a dumb bunny. Well, at least he won't have *her* either."

"I'm the one who urged him to confess," Sidney said softly.

"He needed to tell you, but I warned him not to expect forgiveness… at least not right away."

Dana just stared at him.

"You don't get it, do you, Pastor? No, of course not. I don't expect a *man* to understand what a woman feels when her man thinks another woman can do for him what his wife can't. No, y'all just expect us to let it slide, to be good little wifeys when he goes creepin' into somebody else's bed 'cause it's not just women these days. We're supposed to forgive and forget. We're told it's just what *men do* because y'all are dogs! Well, stop insulting dogs, okay?"

Sidney flinched from the verbal arrows her words were shooting at him. Still, if he couldn't reconcile his own behavior, he could at least do all he could to save this relationship.

"I'm not trying to tell you that, and I can imagine how betrayed you must feel right now."

Dana looked at him as if she could see his own sins.

"Do you really, Pastor Teal? I don't think you have any idea how I feel right now. It's my mother all over again."

The elevator door opened, and Dana marched out, leaving Sidney standing.

"Go back upstairs, Pastor Teal, and comfort him with scripture because as far as I'm concerned, that's all he's got."

CHAPTER ELEVEN

It was another lazy Sunday afternoon for Yasmin. The morning was spent talking to Ambrose who, as he'd predicted several weeks ago, was sleeping in his office and playing catch-up. They talked for hours as she heard the clack-clack of the keyboard and the creaking of leather as he stretched out those long legs of his.

He'd been gone for a few weeks now, and since then, she'd not set foot inside of Holy Word, and she did not miss it. In fact, she planned on making the journey to Harlem to attend Abyssinian Baptist Church. She'd felt something stir in her soul from just touching the stones of the building. It felt real, whereas Holy Word felt more like Sidney Teal's personal theater.

Even though Ambrose was three thousand miles away, Yasmin did not feel lonely. She was like a caterpillar emerging into a butterfly. As promised, she spent more time exploring her state when she wasn't working like a dog. She had Ambrose cracking up when she mentioned how many miles she was putting on her Lexus.

It appeared that Ambrose wasn't quite ready for her to forget him. From the time he left, every Monday morning she would be greeted by a glorious bouquet of flowers on her desk. He never sent a card, but when she opened her e-mail, there would be a note from him. Her co-workers, especially the female ones, wanted to know who he was, but Yasmin kept her secrets.

April-Rose was with Ronnie this weekend in New Jersey, meeting his family and friends, and she had revealed to Yasmin that she was sure Ronnie was about to pop the question.

"What do I *say*, Yaz?" her best friend asked, sounding like a nervous school girl rather than a grown ass woman.

"I mean, I know we've been dating a long time and all that, but—"

Yasmin just chuckled.

"You say yes, heifer. Don't make the brother wait too long."

The line went silent for a minute, then April-Rose said, "I kind of feel bad for talking about this when Ambrose is back in L.A."

"Knock it off, girlfriend," Yasmin admonished her.

"One of the best things about having dumped Sidney was that I've learned to enjoy being by myself. Ambrose

140

and I talk every day, but I just don't feel like something's wrong with me 'cause I don't have a man. I've learned how to love *myself*."

She could feel the huge smile on her friend's face.

"You just go, girl! And you're right. The last time I called you, you were in SoHo."

"Well, when you get back from Jersey, I found this great little boutique that sells this season's fashions for almost a steal."

The other woman squealed with delight.

"You bought something, didn't you, heifer?"

Yasmin couldn't help bragging.

"I'm staring at the cutest Kate Spade handbag that I got for sixty bucks, and it ain't no counterfeit. The place has some kind of deal with certain designers to sell off stuff used in trunk shows and stuff, or overstock. It's a small store, but the place is packed."

"Ooh, girl, you make me almost want to tell Ronnie I'm sick," April-Rose teased.

***

Another aspect of spending Sunday doing other things was that Yasmin was beginning to seriously develop her cooking skills. She'd never been a bad cook. After all, she was a Southern girl and had learned to cook from her mother and grandmother, but now she was experimenting with other types of dishes. Just last week, she'd made her first roasted rack of lamb with a mushroom risotto, and it came out pretty damn good if she could say so herself. Tonight's dinner would be chicken cordon bleu with a salad of mixed baby greens and balsamic vinaigrette. Yasmin chuckled to herself. If she kept cooking the way she was, she'd soon be as fat as a house.

***

As promised, Yasmin and April-Rose were right in the thick of the small outlet store, picking through the best of high-end fashions. April-Rose squealed as she held up a black Donna Karan sheath dress that reminded both of them of Audrey Hepburn's classic little black dress from *Breakfast at Tiffany's*. She glanced at the price tag. Her eyes bugged out, so she glanced at it again to make sure she was reading it correctly. Then she let Yasmin see it.

"Is this for real?" she asked. She mouthed the price as Yasmin nodded.

"Well hell, it's going home with me!"

Yasmin looked through the dresses on the rack, but she really didn't see anything she had to have at that point. However, there were several hippy-style cuff bracelets that were calling her name on the accessories counter.

"Let's make a deal," she whispered to Yasmin as a cute Karen Kane box-pleated skirt ended up in the slowly growing pile in her arms.

"We don't mention this place to those heifers at Holy Word. It'd be just like them to come here actin' all ghetto asking for Apple Bottoms."

Yasmin let out a laugh as the two of them shook hands.

"Most of them wouldn't come all this way anyway. You know how bourgeois they think we are."

They spent another hour in the store, and Yasmin found a pair of Rock and Republic jeans that hugged her curves in all the right places, and a sequined Stella McCartney T-shirt to go along with the bracelets. Both women, satisfied with their shopping outing, decided on one of SoHo's many cafés for lunch. As they sat and ate, Yasmin noticed the absence of an engagement ring on her friend's finger. April-Rose noticed the look.

"No, it didn't happen, but the man keeps hinting at it, so it's like he's got something really special planned for tonight. He's taking me to the Cashmere Roost for dinner."

Yasmin whistled through her salade nicoise.

"Nice. That's the place all those uppity types go to."

She remembered suggesting to Sidney once about going there, and he flatly refused, saying they would be recognized immediately the minute they walked in the door. She shook the memory from her mind. She could go there any time she wanted to now.

"Uh oh, I know *that* look. You're thinking about Pastor Playa again, aren't you?"

"Yeah, but not in the *I miss him* sort of way. Just thinking about how much time I wasted being with a man who couldn't really take me anywhere for fear of being seen with me. I asked him to take me to the Cashmere Roost, and he damn near bit my head off."

"What about Ambrose? Isn't it hard having a long-distance relationship?"

Yasmin took a sip of iced tea.

"The strange thing is, April-Rose, it isn't. We talk every day. We send each other e-mails, and he's showing me how to set up a Skype account. But I got to be real with you. I like having my freedom. I'm learning that I don't need a man to make me happy, but if I want to be with one, he's got to come correct."

April-Rose reached out and squeezed her friend's hand.

"I am so proud of you, heifer," she teased.

"You're like a brand new woman, and now I can share all the juicy gossip from what's been going down at church."

"Oh, do tell."

Yasmin grinned eagerly.

"For starters, Sylvester Goodings was in the hospital a few weeks ago after having run into a lamp post."

Yasmin gasped and whispered a quick prayer for his recovery.

"I heard while he was at the hospital that both Dana and the other woman showed up, and the other woman had no idea he was married."

"Oh snap!"

"Oh snap is right, girlfriend. I heard Dana took off that big ol' platinum and diamond rock he bought her and left it on his chest."

"Day-um! That one diamond was about as big as the Statue of Liberty. Do you think she's ever going back to him?"

April-Rose shook her head.

"Dana up and moved to Vancouver but served him divorce papers before she left. Nah, girl. She's not comin' back. That don't surprise me, though. Dana is one of those strong sisters who don't play that mess."

"That's just crazy, but you know what they say. You got to pay to play."

"Sure you right, girl. That's why I want to be sure of Ronnie before I say yes 'cause I'd have to kill him and maybe the hoe he was with," she said with a devious grin.

"Oh, and Pastor Playa has been missing you something bad. Although he tries to fake it, me and Ronnie catch him looking over to where you used to sit."

Yasmin felt nothing when she heard that. It was her past.

"Well, he just needs to get over it before he says or does something suspicious. I have *no* desire to confront Olivia Teal."

"No, you really don't. She's a nice woman. But seriously, Yaz, it's a damn good thing you called it quits. She's the type that would go all Hurricane Katrina and leave a mess of destruction behind her."

April-Rose grimaced.

"I don't know why she'd waste her breath on that man, but she'd rock that church to its foundations like a ten-point earthquake."

***

"I'm home!"

Sidney entered the foyer of his home, hung up his sports coat, and loosened his tie. He didn't expect an answer since Olivia was probably still upstairs packing for their trip. He marched upstairs and was nearly knocked down by Sidney Jr., who jumped into his father's arms, demanding a hug.

"What's goin' on, little man?" Sidney asked, rubbing his son's head.

"I got an A on my spelling test today, Daddy," he bragged.

"The teacher put my paper on the bulletin board and everything, and that dumb old Mike Weatherbee is telling everybody I cheated, but I didn't! I studied real hard."

He ruffled his son's head again.

"I know you did. That boy is just jealous, but you shouldn't say anything mean about him."

Sidney heard the sound of another pair of feet headed toward him. It was Joshua who also jumped into his arms.

"And what have you been up to, sport?" he asked him as he carried both pint-sized bundles up the stairs and to the landing where he lowered them to the floor.

"We're learning algebra," he said with a huge grin.

"It's hard with all those letters that are like numbers, but I'm going to figure it out and get an A too."

He smiled at his son.

"Well then, you can help Daddy when he has to do math 'cause I don't know that much about algebra."

"Uh uh," Joshua said, shaking his head in disbelief.

"Daddies know *everything*, just like mommies do."

Sidney couldn't help but laugh, and the laughter released the tension from days of consoling and counseling a distraught Sylvester Goodings. The man had lost weight, and his eyes were sunken. The poor man looked like death warmed over, and Sidney had gone through several big boxes of Kleenex because of all the tears the man had shed. He had moved out of the brownstone he and Dana had lived in and was staying with his family.

It was hard to offer comfort to a man so broken, and he couldn't help but wonder if he'd end up the same way if his wife ever found out about Yasmin Lewis. It would be worse because she'd take the kids. The thought of

148

never seeing the bright and trusting faces of his children was a punch in the gut and a reality check.

His sons noticed his silence and vacant stare, and they tugged at him to get his attention.

"Daddy, Daddy, are you okay?" asked Joshua, concern in his small childlike voice. Sidney snapped out of his gloomy thoughts and grabbed both boys in a bear hug.

"Daddy is alright, sport, but I've got to go see your mommy. Make sure you both finish your homework before getting on that PlayStation," he warned them mock-sternly.

"We will," both boys chimed and ran down the stairs to finish their homework at the breakfast nook. Sidney headed toward the bedroom, somewhat apprehensive at what he'd find. As he'd initially thought, his wife was busy packing her large rolling suitcase and looking far too satisfied with herself. She looked up, saw him standing in the doorway, and smiled like a Cheshire cat.

"I'm determined to only have this suitcase and garment bag for my nice suits. I want to make certain everyone knows that Pastor Sidney Teal's wife is a reflection of him," Olivia said.

He walked over and gave her a quick kiss on the lips.

149

"I think I have no need to worry about that. You represent Holy Word very well as a pastor's wife. Everyone thinks so."

Olivia ceased packing and regarded her husband curiously.

"So you're not upset that I decided to attend the conference with you?"

"Not at all, sweetheart. I was just surprised because you've told me several times before how the things bore you, and believe me, they *are* boring. But I think it would be a good thing for you to network with other pastors' wives, and you'll be able to tell them about some of the programs at the church you helped to create."

"That's true," she admitted, her suspicions beginning to lessen a little.

"They may have some ideas for more outreach that we hadn't thought about. I heard one church actually has a program for veterans of the Iraq and Afghanistan wars to help them deal with their post-traumatic stress disorder. That sounds like something I think we should do."

Sidney stretched then began to change from work clothes to a pair of sweats and a Morehouse sweatshirt.

"I'm going to the kitchen to see if those little knuckleheads are doing their homework."

"I'll be down there in a few," she said, folding a pair of khaki slacks.

"Dinner is in the oven, and I left Amia in her playpen asleep."

***

For the first time in a while, dinner wasn't a strained affair. Whatever tensions had been happening under the surface seemed to have disappeared, but Olivia wasn't quite so ready to dismiss her intuition off hand.

It was hard to forget how angry he'd been in the car after they'd left the restaurant. The man had a temper, but he seldom showed it. The fact that he seemed to have made peace with her being with him just felt wrong. She hated herself for being so suspicious, but Sidney's behavior wasn't helping much.

She didn't miss his quick glances to his left during his sermons. There was an empty space where Yasmin Lewis used to sit, but she hadn't been in church for several weeks, and no one seemed to know where she was.

"Can I have another hamburger?" Sidney Jr. asked, holding out his plate. Olivia snapped back to reality and with a huge smile, grabbed the tongs and dropped another patty onto the plate.

"That's your second one, little man. Where'd the first one go?"

He patted his stomach.

"In here, Mommy, and it was so good!"

The phone rang, and Sidney rose from the table to get it. Olivia watched him like a hawk as he answered it.

"No, Sylvester. It's okay," she heard him say, knowing it was poor Brother Goodings on the other end. She knew she should have sympathy for his plight, but sometimes a man needed to know there were consequences for cheating. Not every woman was the "stand by your man" type as Dana obviously proved.

Sidney held the phone from his ear and looked at her.

"I'm going into my study, sweetheart, to finish this call."

He grinned hugely at his kids.

"Save Daddy some of that chocolate cream pie, okay?"

CHAPTER TWELVE

Another great day had come to an end as Yasmin kicked off her Tory Burch pumps and took off her fashionable monkey suit, stretching happily as she did so. She went into the bedroom and popped on a pair of yoga pants and a T-shirt.

It seemed so many blessings were finally coming her way, and her eyes had opened to the possibility of a life free from shame. Even though work was often stressful, especially with new clients and deadlines, she relished the faster pace and the chance to show her bosses that she was a sister to be reckoned with. Yasmin was even making plans to get her MBA, though she hadn't told Ambrose yet. She knew he'd be totally supportive. She was determined to make partner in three to four years.

Even though she wasn't officially *with* Ambrose, he called her or sent e-mails every day, which still didn't stop men from paying more attention to her than before. No, that wasn't true. Men had always paid attention to her, but she was too busy being Sidney's plaything to notice.

She went to the kitchen and opened the refrigerator. She'd been craving the leftovers from last night's masterpiece—Italian sausage and ground turkey lasagna that had been so filled with creamy ricotta goodness and mounds of mozzarella cheese that Tony Soprano would marry her with a quickness. While the lasagna warmed up, she made a quick salad of spinach and arugula with walnuts, and poured herself a glass of Shiraz.

When the food was ready, she plated up a huge slice of her handiwork, some of the salad, and took everything into the living room. It was Wednesday night, and thanks to Ambrose, she was totally hooked on BBC America, especially that new show, *Whitechapel*. It was about a modern-day Jack the Ripper. She flipped channels on the remote, loving the crystal-clear picture of the forty-two-inch plasma screen, until she found the program.

When her cell phone rang, she automatically knew who it was and put it on speaker.

"How's my favorite BBC addict?" Ambrose asked, his silky rumble sending a nice flutter between her legs. There was just something about his proper accent that sounded so hot to her ears.

"Getting ready to stuff my face and watch this damn show you've got me hooked on," she answered teasingly.

"I'm not ready for *Doctor Who*. That's just a little too weird for me right now."

There was hearty laughter at the other end.

"Well, Yasmin, here's the deal. You're going to have to become a huge doctor fan if you want to be *my lady.*"

My lady reverberated through her head like an echo.

"If that's all it takes, then I guess I need to start Googling to play catchup."

"Start with season two," he suggested.

"The doctor's companion, Rose, is black. I think you'll dig that."

Yasmin chewed a forkful of lasagna and swallowed it.

"Do they get to get their freak on? I notice a lot of these English shows have interracial couples who get to do more than kiss."

"That's true, but then again, most of Europe isn't in the dark ages when it comes to that kind of thing. When I was over there, I saw quite a few mixed couples. By the way, did you get those pictures I sent you?"

"You mean of that black woman who's the Crown Princess of Lichtenstein? I didn't even know there was such a country. How come they never reported that over here?"

Yasmin could envision Ambrose's raised eyebrow.

"Now why on earth would the American media ever want to report something positive like that? Just think of

155

all the little black girls who would see a real life princess and not the Disney version."

For some reason, the talk of interracial relationships made her ask, "Have you dated a woman who wasn't a sister?"

Ambrose didn't hesitate.

"I have; a couple of times, in fact. More like friendly than serious, but yes. This isn't an issue for you, is it?"

Yasmin swallowed, not sure of how to answer him without sounding accusing.

"I kind of guessed that you had. It makes sense, considering what you do and where you live. Seems like most successful black men go that way."

"Yes, I guess it does seem that way, given the media's fixation, but a lot of my black co-workers are married to beautiful accomplished black women. To tell the truth, a few of my white co-workers are too."

Yasmin gasped, having never really considered that as an option.

"I'd hate to think that I'd never even be thought of as someone you could be with just because I wasn't black."

She hesitated.

"I don't know. I don't think white guys pay me any attention."

Ambrose chuckled.

"Are you kidding me? I've seen guys of all colors check you out. You are a gorgeous woman with class, style, and smarts. What man *wouldn't* want you? No matter what color I am, if I saw you walking down the street, I'd do everything I could to catch up to you and ask you out."

That made her smile like an idiot.

***

Later that night, Yasmin soaked in her bathtub. The water was hot and soothing as she leaned her head back on her bath pillow.

She hadn't even paid attention to all the mayhem on the screen. Talking to Ambrose had been much more important. For the millionth time, she thanked God, April-Rose, Ronnie, in that order, for having brought Ambrose Hunter into her life.

She had never felt so at ease with anyone other than her best friend, and even though Ambrose had so many experiences and knew so many things, he never once made her feel stupid. If anything, he made her want to be as curious and as open-minded as he was. She even noticed how she was using less slang in her conversations. She knew she didn't *have* to change for a man, but for this one, she wanted to be the kind of woman that had always been inside of her.

She knew her family would most definitely approve of Ambrose once they got over his way of talking and his mannerisms. He was a black man with a good job, no bad habits that she knew about, wasn't gay, on drugs, or with a white woman, though he admitted he'd dated them in the past. Once she thought about it, it didn't bother her as much as she thought it might. In short, he was just right.

Yasmin just couldn't believe how happy she was. Even though he was far away, she felt that she could trust Ambrose. That was a feeling she hadn't had in who knew how long. April-Rose had told her he was a one-woman man and a hopeless romantic. She no longer cared about Sidney or all the drama that had once been a part of her life with him.

Her mama's warning came to her from out of the blue. She'd heard it said many times to family members from her mother's mouth. *Be careful of what you do and how you treat others in this life, chile, for your deeds will certainly find you out.*

It had been months since she'd seen or heard from him, but a small part of her wondered if or when the axe

158

would fall. It didn't help things much that, according to April-Rose, the man kept glancing in the direction where she used to sit. Didn't he know how to keep things on the down low? Was the idiot trying to destroy his marriage *and* his ministry? She'd long since moved on and no longer had anything to feel guilty about.

Not true, came the voice of her conscience. What would happen if Ambrose ever found out what she'd been like before she met him and that she'd been sleeping with a married man? Just thinking about that troubled her. She felt dirty and ashamed. The only thing she could do was to swear that nothing would ever happen between her and Sidney Teal ever again.

CHAPTER THIRTEEN

Friday afternoon found Sidney shuffling papers at his desk. The Tennessee trip was fast approaching, and he wanted to tie up all loose ends. He'd been looking forward to spending time with Yasmin. That was until she told him to get lost. Now he'd be forced to attend with Olivia, who just couldn't shut up about how excited she was about the conference.

No, he wasn't being fair to his wife. Maybe Olivia was trying to change to make more room for him in her life. He owed it to her to try and make things better. He was also torn up over Brother Goodings, who was still very out of it. He couldn't even say Dana's name without breaking down into tears. Sidney had never seen any man so broken, and he couldn't help putting himself in the other man's place.

It would be worse because not only was his marriage on the line, but everything he'd built—his reputation, and his ministry—Olivia would destroy it all. What she would do to Yasmin was anyone's guess.

He tried to make himself see that his affair with Yasmin had been an aberration, a weakness. He tried to take Ross's advice to let it go. Instead, all he saw was

161

Yasmin looking like a tempting chocolate bar that he just had to nibble on.

With a dreamy smile, he remembered the few times he'd had her in his office. Oh, she'd been a little firecracker back then, trying to squirm from his embrace but knowing she really wanted him too. How many times had the two of them skirted the edge of danger? Of course, it had made the sex between them explosive.

He couldn't even imagine Olivia being that bold now. Before the children and before the status of being a preacher's wife kicked in, she would have. But now, she'd fight him off, worried about the creases in her Chanel suit.

Sidney realized with a pang of guilt that he was being harsh. How many times had he told the married men he counseled that women change after having children? That sex was still important, but they were tired from often being a working woman and a mother, and that the best way to get your wife in the mood was to help around the house and help with the kids? Some of them took his advice. Others spurned it, saying that housework was for women. He didn't miss the irony about taking his own advice.

It was time to let it go and do everything he could to get his marriage back on track. He could dismiss the whole thing with Yasmin as a lesson learned and move on. Besides, she wasn't around to tempt him with that face and that body.

His cell phone rang.

"Hi, honey. I was calling to see what time you'll be home tonight. The boys wanted pizza for dinner, so I wanted to know should I order it now or wait 'til you're close by."

"Go ahead and order it, and I'll pick it up on my way in," Sidney said, thinking of his adorable and very hungry little boys and little Amia, who could destroy a pizza before stuffing the entire thing into her mouth.

"I'm wrapping up everything as we speak. Brother Goodings is spending time with his brother in Chicago. I pray it will help him get back on his feet."

"Amen," his wife intoned.

"I'm glad you and Ross were there for him."

"Me too. It's times like this one knows who they can turn to in times of troubles, but also who their real friends are."

"Well, I'll see you in a bit, honey," Olivia said as he heard the unmistakable sound of boys being boys in the background.

"I think I've got a wrestling match to decide."

After he hung up, he thought of what he'd said to his wife about knowing who one's real friends were. Outside of Ross, who would stick with *him* should the truth ever come to light? It was true what they said about it being lonely at the top. Who would lead the church after his fall from grace? What would they do with it and all the community outreach programs he'd started with Olivia by his side? Would there be a mass defection like he'd seen happen with other churches when scandal hit them?

He felt a little guilty for thinking more about Holy Word than he did about his family, but Sidney had always been able to compartmentalize his feelings until now. But he did care about what would happen to his children. What would Olivia tell them? Worse, what would they hear from strangers?

Sidney had to keep his eyes on the prize. It was over between him and Yasmin, and he had to accept that. It was easier said than done, and he wondered if she felt the same.

***

It was another one of those picture perfect Southern California days—blue skies with a hint of ocean breeze and the temperature hovering somewhere around the upper seventies. It was one of those days that Ambrose wished he could show Yasmin, as he drove her around the city he'd called home for most of his life.

Instead, he was stuck indoors in business casual chinos, a button-down shirt, a sweater vest with Cole-Hahn leather loafers, a mountain of files on his desk, and a computer monitor ringed with sticky notes. Several thick law books laid open in front of him.

He was busy, but not busy enough to take a break and call Yasmin or send her a quick text. He knew she was getting the flowers he'd sent every Monday, and he loved the cute squeal of surprise when she called to thank him.

He had no idea when he went to visit Ronnie that he was going to meet a woman as amazing as Yasmin Lewis. He hadn't been planning on meeting any female after the disaster that had been Janelle and her thug boyfriend on the side. Amazingly, her betrayal didn't hurt as much, but he was still inclined to be cautious. Then again, Yasmin somehow had gotten under his skin in a relatively short amount of time, and although they still had that distance part to work out, Ambrose was positive *they* could make it work.

Later that evening, while he was relaxing with some Middle Eastern trance music his executive secretary, Zahra, had introduced him to, his phone rang.

"Yo, my man," came Ronnie's booming voice.

"How's my favorite cousin? Still out there on the ocean trying to get eaten by Jaws?"

Ambrose just laughed. It was a running joke between the two of them.

"Unfortunately, things have been insane at the firm, and I haven't felt like getting up at the crack of dawn, so I don't get to be shark bait for a while."

"So, are you still hollering at Yasmin Lewis?"

From anyone else, Ambrose would have given a quick answer then changed the subject, but Ronnie was more like a brother than a cousin, and they'd always kept each other's secrets.

"That's another reason I'm so tired. We talk every night for hours. She's an amazing woman."

He heard his cousin clear his throat, and the line went silent for a few seconds.

"I've got a confession to make."

Ambrose's heart suddenly sped up.

"If you tell me she's married, I will *kill* you."

"No, nothing like that."

Ronnie's voice cracked a little.

"I was hesitant about introducing you to her at first because well... you're not exactly... well... you know?"

Ambrose *did* know, and that was one of the reasons Janelle gave for cheating on him. He didn't quite understand why his blackness was always in question just because he didn't fit a certain stereotype. He refused to dumb himself down for anyone. He'd worked too damn hard to get to where he was, and if some people couldn't handle him being an individual first and a black man second, that was on them. He hoped Yasmin wouldn't turn out to be that way. So far, she hadn't.

"Anyway," Ronnie continued, cutting into his thoughts.

"April-Rose was all over me to hook you two up. She thought you two might hit it off, and well, you did."

"Is that it?"

"Well, no. You see, my woman wanted Yasmin to start seeing someone who had something going for him because she certainly wasn't meeting those kinds of men at her job, and forget about those losers at that church she used to go to. Man, talk about drama. Some Sundays it's like Oprah meets T.D. Jakes."

"So what changed your mind about me?"

"She did. April-Rose says that she's never seen her girlfriend so damn happy. All she talks about is Ambrose this and Ambrose that, and frankly, cuz, I'm sick of hearing about how great you are. If you weren't related to me, the beatdown would be on," Ronnie joked.

The two men laughed, especially knowing that Ambrose had whipped his cousin's butt several times when they were kids because Ronnie had called him an "Oreo." Like most family members, they'd gotten over it and been tight ever since.

On the other end of the line, Ronnie hated himself for lying to his cousin, but it wasn't his place to say anything. Besides, there was no need to, according to April-Rose, since Yasmin had long since given Pastor Playa his walking papers. Everybody was happy, at least everybody who mattered. Still, he felt a twinge of remorse and hoped like hell that Yasmin Lewis didn't do anything to mess up this good thing. He didn't give a damn if she was his lady's best friend. Ambrose was his cousin, and blood was thicker than water.

CHAPTER FOURTEEN

Olivia watched intently as her husband applied his John Varvatos Star USA cologne. The woodsy scent tickled her nostrils. A lot of men didn't know how to wear cologne. For that matter, neither did a lot of women. Sidney splashed on just enough to linger lightly.

Times like this where she watched him, she found herself falling in love with him all over again. He was a fine specimen of a man. That she had to admit. It wasn't too hard to understand why so many women envied her. Sidney took very good care of himself, exercising an hour every day to keep fit and to maintain health. He got facials and manicures like she did, but no one should get it twisted that he was soft. He enjoyed taking care of himself because he was always in the public eye, and he knew she appreciated it.

Daydreaming like this made whatever suspicions she'd harbored seem unreal. She caught the glimmer of the wide solid gold wedding band on his left finger, and her heart skipped a beat. There were times she still had to pinch herself knowing he belonged to her, which was why she tried to do everything possible to keep their marriage strong. Watching him pack, she thought back to the conversation between herself, Mother Teal, and Sister Mary, and decided to take her mother-in-law's wise advice. She would *not* allow anyone to come between her and her husband. By the time this trip was over, Sidney Teal wouldn't give another woman a second thought. She thought wickedly about the fun little toys she'd purchased from an online adult toys catalog that she'd packed. She couldn't wait to try the cherry-flavored love lotion on him.

"Livvy, honey," Sidney called, snapping her out of her trance.

"I asked have you seen my black jeans."

"Oh, yes," Olivia replied with a mysterious smile on her creamy features.

"I picked them up from the cleaners earlier. They should be in your closet."

Sidney found the missing pants, folded them neatly, and then placed a brief but warm kiss on her cheek.

"Thinking about our trip?" he asked.

She nodded.

"I think going together is a good thing for us. I realize that it's been about the kids and the church, but we both could use some private time, right?"

Sidney nodded, really and truly wanting to believe that. Maybe it wasn't too late to save his marriage. Maybe Olivia was turning over a new leaf. He most certainly planned to. He bent over and kissed her lips again.

"You're right, honey. I'm glad that you decided to come along. Just think."

He folded her into a strong embrace.

"No rambunctious boys with their even more rambunctious sister in tow. Just you and me."

***

Olivia had expected Amia to throw a tantrum before they left, but she smiled and waved while holding Chantel Tindal's hand. The boys tried their best to behave like brave little men, but Joshua's bottom lip quivered, and Mommy gave him an extra hug.

"Now you be good and do what Auntie Chantel says," she admonished them gently.

"That means no chocolate before bedtime, and the PlayStation is off at 8:00 p.m. sharp."

"Yes, Mommy," they said in unison. Chantel had made herself at home, and the kids loved her. Both Olivia and Sidney knew they were leaving their precious children in good hands.

"I'll even make sure they eat their veggies," she said as Sidney Jr. wrinkled his nose. He hated anything that was green and good for him.

Olivia gave them all one more hug then she got into the airport shuttle bus where her husband was already waiting. She was of mixed emotions, already missing them and yet excited for the first time in a long time that she'd finally be taking some much needed 'me' time with her husband. The kids would be fine. Chantel and Ross were wonderful friends, and her kids couldn't have been left in better hands.

***

It had been quite some time since she'd traveled, and Sidney had been right about getting to the airport a few hours in advance. The check-in part had been relatively quick. It was the security screening that seemed to take forever as the line snaked around several turnstiles and people moved slowly. She was glad she'd worn the sensible and comfortable Toms slip-ons.

Finally, they boarded the plane and were instantly directed to first class. Olivia's eyes widened in surprise as Sidney grinned at her.

"This is how *I* like to travel. I think you'll enjoy it too."

"Would you care for something to drink?" the flight attendant asked them both politely. Sidney took his wife's hand.

"Yes, I think two glasses of white wine would be nice."

The flight attendant poured the drinks then rolled the cart down the aisle. He held his glass for a toast.

"To new beginnings."

***

The Marquee Hotel was exquisite with plush carpeting, expensive paintings and fresh cut flowers in practically every available space. The hotel was packed to capacity with church folks from nearly all over the country, and from a few foreign countries as well. From a distance, Olivia spied Prophetess Juanita Bynum, who carried herself with grace and class in spite of everything that had happened to her. It had been sad how many sisters had turned on the woman they'd once considered a friend simply because she didn't feel like being any man's punching bag. That reminded her of the conversation she'd had in the kitchen with Sister Jordan. Some women would take a lot of mess to keep the peace and not to let out dirty laundry. *She* wasn't one of those women.

"Oh, Sidney!"

Their room was magnificent with a beautiful view of the city. The attached bedroom had a king-sized bed, plush chairs, and carpeting so soft that it was like walking on air. As she walked around the suite, the bellhop discreetly knocked on the door with their luggage. He wheeled everything in and neatly placed them in the bedroom.

"Will that be all, sir?" he asked smartly as Sidney tipped him generously.

"Thank you, son, but I think we're all good here."

"Well, enjoy your stay, and if you need anything, my name is Kevin."

With that, he closed the door behind him. Sidney stretched. The flight hadn't been too long, but it was nice to stretch one's legs. The evening belonged to them since the conference didn't officially start until tomorrow. He decided to take a quick shower, and perhaps he and Olivia would order room service.

The minute he walked into the semi-darkened bedroom, he stopped in his tracks. Olivia was lying seductively beneath the sheet which barely covered her perfect café au lait breasts tipped with nipples the color of

174

almond drops. He moved closer to her, taking in the outline of her beautiful body.

"Livvy," his deep masculine voice groaned as he pulled down the sheet exposing her sexy body. He chuckled erotically.

"I was going to order room service, but I guess I can do that any time. Come here, woman."

He gathered her in his powerful embrace and closed his eyes as he savored the feel of silk against his body. God, it had been so long. She wasn't Yasmin, but dammit, she didn't have to be. This sexy woman writhing against him shamelessly was the woman he'd married, and if he were honest with himself, the woman he still did love.

Shedding his clothes with a quickness, he kissed her until she was begging him to be inside of her, and Sidney was more than willing to comply. He entered her gently but firmly as he moved slow and deep then picked up the pace. He rocked her slowly then faster then slowly again, making her body tremble with heated desire.

"Say my name," he demanded pumping into her harder and deeper as she wrapped her beautiful thighs around his hips.

"Say it. Say it," he demanded again.

"Oh, Sidney! Sidney!" Olivia cried out in ecstasy as they both came crashing down like waves in a blistering storm. They both panted heavily as they smiled like two people who'd just rocked each other's worlds. Their breathing slowed as silence fell between them, and sleep took over their shimmering bodies.

The only thing to mar the perfect moment for a split second before he came was that he looked down and saw Yasmin's face.

**

Olivia woke to the sound of Sidney singing in the shower. It had been a long time since she'd heard his glorious baritone outside of church. She loved hearing him sing.

Last night had been everything and more that she could have ever hoped for. They ordered room service, talked in a way they hadn't in a while, then made love again slowly. Olivia winced a bit at the pounding she'd taken at her sexy husband's hands, but she had no complaints.

Time to get up myself, she thought, knowing she'd have a full day and wouldn't see much of Sidney until later. That was okay too because she really was looking forward to fellowshipping with the other pastors' wives.

Holy Word had quite the reputation for community outreach programs, but there was always room for more. She also knew that she might have to defend their decision to take on the HIV/AIDS crisis in their community head-on. Some churches still ignored it as if the disease would skip them somehow, but she believed that knowledge was power and that the black community had to be proactive when it came to dealing with it.

***

"I am so glad that we finally get to meet, Mrs. Teal. I've heard a lot about you and your husband's work at Holy Word. I think it's a model for the modern church."

The effusive compliment came from Dr. Lynette Crane, a pastor at Healing Hope Church located in San Francisco. Dr. Crane herself was famous, or infamous, for espousing social justice along with the gospel, and her church was truly a rainbow coalition. She often participated in conferences and seminars geared toward male pastors, something that upset some of the more traditional-minded. She was most interested in what pastors' wives, whom she believed were just as instrumental in the church, were doing.

Olivia glowed like a firefly at the praise, and she admired a woman who was willing to take on the powers that be to spread the gospel.

"Believe me. It took some doing, and initially, we lost some of our members, but Sidney and I believe that the black church needs to stay important in people's lives, especially the lives of young adults. We need to make Jesus relevant to their daily lives and not just some concept hanging from a cross."

"Amen, my sister." The other woman agreed.

"The church has lost so many of our young people because it has failed to speak to them. Worse, we've allowed too many with hate in their hearts, who pretend to love the Lord, to do all the talking for us."

"It's an uphill battle, but every day I feel the spirit telling me what we do at Holy Word is right. The next thing Sidney and I are working on is attracting more men back to church."

Dr. Crane squeezed her hand.

"I have no doubt that you both will come up with something that works, and believe me, I'll be watching. It was wonderful meeting you, and here's my card."

She pulled out an elegant foiled business card, handing it to Olivia.

"Let's definitely keep in touch."

It was nearly six in the evening when Olivia made it back to the hotel room. She was as giddy as a schoolgirl, having met so many wonderful and open people who were all devoted to serving the Lord. She wondered why she'd never come to one of these conferences before. Well, she had no plans to stay away from now on.

She knew that Sidney probably wouldn't be back until a little later and decided to take a nice warm shower to relax. Just maybe he would come in and surprise her. She definitely felt her sexy back. Kicking off her heels, she undressed in the bedroom then padded nude into the marble-tiled bathroom.

Olivia closed her eyes as the warm water rained upon her flawless butter-nut skin. Yes, it had been a highly productive first day. It was nice to meet other pastors' wives who weren't content to sit around and be ornaments. Most had doctorates or worked outside the home, something that surprised her but something she had long been considering.

"Livvy?"

She heard the door open then close. Her stomach fluttered with excitement, hoping that he would find her here, naked, wet, and waiting for him. The bathroom door opened.

"Is there room for two in there?"

CHAPTER FIFTEEN

Ambrose was putting in fourteen- to sixteen-hour days because he had plans. He said nothing to Yasmin as they talked, but at the same time, he was making reservations for a surprise trip to New York for the weekend.

There was a part of him that urged caution. Though Janelle was history, that voice inside of him warned that he might be going too fast. He silenced it by convincing himself that he was just going to visit Yasmin as a friend, which was true.

He wasn't going to say anything to his cousin either. In spite of how supportive Ronnie appeared to be about his growing relationship with Yasmin, he also had the feeling that Ronnie might have been worried about something. Then again, Ronnie had always worried about him when it came to women.

That was another reason for the visit. He wanted to find out how she felt about getting in deeper, such as in a long-distance relationship. It was something he'd been considering for quite some time and knew the pros and cons. He did not expect her to give up her life and her job for him. Of course, there was the trust issue as well.

Even if she said no, he still wanted her as a friend. He really enjoyed her company and her down-to-earth attitude. She was smart, sassy, and he had to admit, a fine woman who took care of herself, but not overly vain. She was the type of independent woman who took care of herself, and women like that always turned him on.

Her skin always smelled so good. It wasn't the perfumes she wore, but it was something uniquely Yasmin Lewis. It was fresh and clean yet sweet too.

Just thinking about her reaction to *Law and Order UK* made him smile again, and in spite of the daunting workload, he found himself whistling a silly tune. He hadn't felt this good in quite some time.

***

Olivia threw her arms around her children, who hugged her back with giggles and smiles on their sweet little faces. Amia had one of her favorite picture books under her arm.

"I wan' to tell you a night-night story, Mommy," she said with pride in her little voice. Chantel chuckled.

"That's all she's been doing is grabbing books and reading by herself. I think I've heard *Princess Tianna's*

Big Surprise at least ten times."

"It's a icky princess book," complained Joshua.

"She doesn't want to read about sports or dragons."

Just being with her children again made Olivia's jet lag disappear entirely. Like every mother, she listened attentively to their adventures while she and their father were away. She laughed when she was supposed to, felt sympathy, and gave reassuring hugs and kisses when those were called for. She even dished out discipline when it was needed. Chantel sat next to Amia, nodding all the while.

After they'd been sent upstairs, Olivia gave her friend a heartfelt hug and opened her purse, presenting an elegantly-wrapped box.

"I just wanted you to know how much I appreciated you staying with the children," she explained as Chantel carefully undid the ribbon. When she opened the box, her eyes grew misty, holding out a dainty gold bracelet.

"You didn't have to do this, Olivia."

Her hand shook as she fastened the bracelet around her slender wrist. In the light of the late-afternoon sun, it shimmered brightly.

"It's beautiful. Thank you so much."

Looking at Olivia, who seemed different, happier, she

184

couldn't help asking, "Was it a good trip?"

Olivia gave her a wicked wink. "Oh girlfriend, you haven't any idea just how *good* it was."

After Chantel left, Olivia went upstairs, still riding high on all the good feelings from her children and her husband. She and Sidney had needed this trip to reconnect as husband and wife, not as parents or the leaders of Holy Word. It was more than just the lovemaking, though she certainly had no complaints on *that* score. It was about spending time, talking about their hopes and dreams, sharing laughs, and feeling blessed to have so much.

She was determined to take Mother Teal's advice and do everything possible to strengthen their marriage. She was certain her suspicions were just in her mind. Why else would Sidney have rocked her body six ways 'til Sunday and treated her like a queen the rest of the time?

With that resolve, she headed upstairs. She'd worry about unpacking tomorrow.

***'

This was Sidney's first Saturday with absolutely nothing to do. He could stay home and enjoy a peaceful morning with a newspaper and a cup of coffee. He watched Olivia making blueberry pancakes, the sun playing gently with her honey almond skin.

After Tennessee, he had become the perfect husband. He'd done his best to treat her with the utmost love and respect that she deserved, in spite of Yasmin Lewis. That was why he was doing everything he could to forget his affair and start over again.

The boys rushed down the stairs, followed by Amia, who was at the age where she wanted to try everything they did and wasn't too concerned about falling down.

"Yay, blueberry pancakes," Sidney Jr. announced with a toothy smile lighting up his face.

"I'm hungry!"

"Me too," said both Joshua and Amia as they hugged their mother who was artfully flipping pancakes onto a platter. She kissed them back.

"Go wash up now. And don't forget we're going to the zoo today."

Olivia looked over at her handsome husband and her three beautiful children. She was so thankful to God for having so much happiness in her life. Ever since that trip to Tennessee, it was as if Sidney was a brand-new man altogether. *Yes*, she thought to herself with a smile. *That trip was exactly what we needed.*

Sidney was lost in another world, thinking about his

mistress and how she once made him blueberry pancakes, and just the image of her with that cute speck of batter on her nose that he'd kissed away, which had led to breakfast being put on hold for an hour or so, did nothing for his resolve. He stood up quickly, and when Olivia looked at him with a questioning expression, he gave her a reassuring smile.

"I want to check on Brother Goodings, sweetheart," he told her as he planted a quick kiss on her lips.

"I won't be but a minute, and then," he announced to his children who were busy dumping tons of syrup on their small stacks, "we go to the zoo!"

"I wanna see a 'lephant," said Amia, carefully trying to shove a forkful of pancake into her mouth.

"An' I wanna see Arthur."

When he looked at Olivia for assistance, she laughed.

"Arthur's a cartoon aardvark, and she loves him almost as much as she does Elmo. One day when you're home with the kids, I'll make you sit and watch the show."

Pinching the chubby cheek, he beamed down at his youngest.

"I'll be right back."

The moment he was out of sight, he took his cell

phone from his pants pocket, his hands shaking with nervous excitement. He just wanted to hear her voice and to see if she was all right. He wanted to know if she missed him as much as he tried not to miss her. Closing the door to his study, he speed-dialed Yasmin's number.

"Sidney?"

She sounded surprised.

"Hello, Yasmin. How are you?"

"I'm doing just fine. Why are you calling me?"

"No reason. I just haven't seen you at church in a while and wondered if you were okay."

The sigh on the other end was one of annoyance.

"Sidney, it's over. I don't know how much clearer I can make it, but we're done. Dammit, I meant to get a new cell phone."

"I miss you, baby," he said softly.

"Just stop. You don't miss me, and you don't love me. Why can't you understand that what we had was wrong and let it go? I have, and I'm happy. Besides, why would I continue attending Holy Word when you're there? I've made a new start, and you should do the same. Now, goodbye."

The call ended with an abrupt *click*. Sidney stood for some time, just holding the phone in his hands. She didn't

188

mean it. She couldn't have. But if she did, maybe they could still be friends. Sidney was certain he could still have Yasmin in his life, perhaps just not as a lover. He would go and talk to her again, maybe get her to come back to Holy Word. He'd even accept that she had a new man.

Snatching up his car keys, he dashed from the study to the kitchen, schooling his face into a worried expression. When his wife saw it, she immediately went into concerned mode.

"Brother Goodings okay, honey?"

"The man is fragile," he told her sorrowfully.

"I'm going to go see him for a minute, but I won't be gone too long. Darn, and I was hoping to have a day off with my family." He sighed for emphasis. Olivia simply kissed him and patted him on the shoulder.

"Go do what you can for the man," she said encouragingly.

"If you want, I'll take the kids to the zoo, and you can meet us there."

"No, just wait for me."

He kissed her again.

"Livvy, what would I do without you? I'll be right back."

Turning to his worried children, he gave them a reassuring smile.

"Daddy won't miss the zoo, and I won't miss seeing Arven."

"Arthur," Amia corrected him in the way a two-year-old could.

"His name is Arthur, Daddy."

He laughed.

"Right, Arthur. Well, I'll be back and then we can go see him. Okay?"

Olivia watched her husband as he pulled out of the driveway. The expression on his face scared her a little. *Something is definitely wrong with Brother Goodings*, she thought as she slowly ate her own breakfast. She truly felt sorry for the young man, in spite of his transgressions. He must have loved Dana very much to be mourning the ending of their marriage. On the other hand, what on earth did he expect to happen? There were many young women like Dana in the church who demanded absolute fidelity from the men they married and whom weren't willing to put up with anything less. Perhaps this was a good thing for men to realize there were indeed consequences, and that when they made vows in front of the Lord, they were expected to keep them.

"Okay, guys, go finish getting cleaned up so that when Daddy comes back, we can head off to the zoo," she ordered them as she rinsed off the dishes and put them into the dishwasher. They scrambled off to do as she told them, little voices high-pitched with excitement.

Once the dishwasher was loaded and running, she set off to the bedroom to put on jeans and a brightly-printed blouse. On the way, she heard Sidney's cell phone ringing in the study and was shocked. The call must have been serious because Sidney *never* forgot his phone. The thing was nearly attached to him.

Entering the study, she saw Sylvester Goodings' name and number beaming on the screen, and she answered it.

"Brother Goodings, how are you? Sidney is on his way, and I guess he forgot his phone."

"I'm managing, Mrs. Teal. It's a struggle every day, but I'm managing. You said he's on his way?"

"Yes, he sped out of here just a minute ago on his way to see you."

"But I'm not in the city," Sylvester told her, and Olivia's heart sped up.

"I've been in Chicago with my family for a while, and I wanted to let him know when I'd be back."

"Oh, okay," she said, confused.

"There must be an honest explanation," she said with a feeling she didn't want to have.

"I'll tell him, and Brother Goodings, I'll keep you in my prayers."

"Thank you, Mrs. Teal. I appreciate that."

Once the call ended, Olivia just stared at the phone wondering just what the hell was going on. Sidney lied to her? No, that couldn't be it. Maybe she heard wrong, that he was on his way to see about Brother Goodings, not to actually *see* him. Maybe he was headed to see Ross Tindal or one of the other deacons.

The phone beckoned her seductively. It would be so easy to push one button and find out what she didn't really want to know. No, she couldn't do that. Their marriage was built on trust. She'd once harbored suspicions, and those suspicions had almost ruined her relationship, but after Tennessee, everything was better now. It had to be.

Five minutes went by, then ten, then fifteen, and she stood there in his study holding the phone. Should she, or shouldn't she?

Sidney would never know, she told herself as she began checking recent calls. He'd never know about her

192

lapse of trust. It was when one name came up once, then twice, then more that Olivia's heart finally broke.

Yasmin Lewis's name and number were right there in front of her. *Oh God.*

***

Sidney sped down the highway, thinking of Yasmin and thinking, *what the hell am I doing*? Why couldn't he accept that she'd moved on? Why was he still seeing her face and feeling her kisses when he should have been concentrating on Olivia? Why was he tempting fate? Was Ross right that he was obsessed? Was this God's punishment on him, or was the enemy putting lust in his heart and making him risk his marriage, his family, and everything he worked for?

Sidney felt a tear slide down his cheek. Was it possible that he really was in love with Yasmin Lewis after all? Dear God, it couldn't be possible. He was a married man, a God-fearing man with a thriving ministry. He had wealth and prestige. He had a wife who adored him and children for whom he was a hero in their eyes. People looked to him for spiritual guidance and leadership. He wondered what his congregation would think if they could see him now, entangled with a woman with whom he'd no ties to other than sex but who had since moved on with her life. Sidney lowered his head in shame as he asked an even more important question. What about the relationship he had with his almighty God?

CHAPTER SIXTEEN

Ambrose stopped on his way to Yasmin's apartment and picked up a bouquet of pink and red roses, a bottle of Pinot Grigio, and a mile away, he called for take-out from a Chinese food restaurant that the two of them had eaten at before and liked.

His heart was racing a mile a minute. He hadn't done anything this spontaneous in a long time, but he found that he liked it. He hoped Yasmin was home and hoped that she'd be happy to see him. He did come bearing gifts after all. He grinned like a madman to himself.

The plan in his mind was a nice dinner and a relaxing evening watching some of the movies he'd brought. He was determined to make a *Matrix* fan out of her yet. There were no thoughts of anything after that, but he definitely wanted to know where her mind was as far as any relationship between them was concerned. Okay, so he was a little old-fashioned, and though the idea of sex had occurred to him, that just wasn't how he operated. Another thing Janelle had held against him was that he treated women with respect. He was sure Yasmin appreciated that.

Pulling up to her apartment building, he noticed a

black Escalade parked nearby and thought nothing of it as he grabbed the roses, the wine, and the bag filled with delicious Chinese goodies, including the dim sum that he remembered she liked. He thought at that moment to call first, but he really wanted to surprise her like a little kid wanted to surprise his parents with something nice.

As Ambrose climbed the stairs, he heard raised voices, one of which sounded like Yasmin's, and he raced upwards to see what was happening or if she was in trouble.

"Tell me again, Yasmin, that it's over," a deep male voice demanded, and Ambrose paused for a second, waiting expectantly for a reply.

"Sidney, it's over! I don't know how many times I have to say that. What's it going to take before you finally leave me in peace?"

"I don't believe you, Yasmin. We had something special," the male voice continued, pleading. Ambrose heard the catch in her voice.

"No, what we had was *sex*. Sex between two people who shouldn't have started anything in the first place, and I should have known better. You were married, and there was no future for us."

Ambrose reached the landing where Yasmin stood in

jeans, a T-shirt, and bare feet. In front of her, a tall distinguished, dark-skinned man spun around to see him. Her eyes went wide.

"Ambrose," she breathed, and he heard the absolute panic, knowing he'd heard the exchange. He just stood there, holding his packages and feeling as if the entire world had just caved in on him, and then he pivoted.

"Ambrose, wait!"

When she tried to reach him, all he could do was pull away. It was the Janelle drama all over again. Ambrose put his brain on pause, dropped the flowers and the bag of food, but kept the wine, knowing he was probably going to need it. He didn't say a word. He just walked calmly and coldly back down the stairs, got in his rental, and sped off.

***

Yasmin looked down to see the beautiful bouquet resting in a heap on the stairs, and the smell of the food just made her ill. She looked at the mess, at Sidney, and down the stairs where she heard Ambrose's car taking off like a bat out of hell.

She stooped down, picked up the roses and the bag of food, turned, and went inside. She felt Sidney follow her, and she just didn't care. She didn't care that he'd slipped his arms around her or that his mouth was on hers. She didn't care that he'd undressed her or laid her down on the bed. She felt nothing as he moved inside of her... did not hear his declarations of love. All she saw was the look of pain on Ambrose's face. The day of reckoning had come.

When Sidney finally left, having used her shower to wash away his crime, Yasmin buried her head in her pillow and wept until the pillow was soaked and there were no more tears to cry.

***

Sidney pulled into his driveway with thoughts of Yasmin revolving in his mind. He didn't know why he'd made love to her once more. She just wasn't even there. She'd laid in the bed like someone in a coma, and no amount of the expertise that had once had her begging for more had been enough to rouse her. Still, he couldn't stop himself. That lack of self-control made him hate himself even more.

Looking down at his silver Rolex, he noticed the time. All that had happened, and he'd only been gone for two hours. There would be plenty of time for the zoo, and since he'd showered before leaving Yasmin's, there would be nothing to give him away. It didn't even bother him that he'd discovered he'd left his cell phone at home since Olivia seldom went into his study. He would put on his dutiful husband face and make the best of a disastrous day. The only good thing, and he felt horrible for thinking such, was that the new man in Yasmin's life was no longer a concern, given the disgusted look he'd seen in the brother's eyes.

But when he went inside and the house was strangely quiet, Sidney had a sinking feeling that all was not as it should have been. Olivia sat stone-faced as Sidney entered the family room. She had her arms folded across her chest as her eyes found his. He glanced down, saw his cell phone in her manicured hands, and knew his own reckoning had finally come.

"Livvy, where are the kids?" he asked, looking directly at her. "We are going to the zoo, aren't we?"

"The children are next door with Mr. and Mrs. Clark," she said coldly.

"I could ask where you've been, but you'd only lie to me."

"I went to see Brother Goodings," he began, but she held up her hand, the one with his cell phone in it.

"No you didn't. Right after you left, he called to tell you that he was still in *Chicago* with his family."

199

Sidney waited for the storm to hit, but Olivia remained implacable in her silence, her eyes filled with a cold rage. He'd never been so afraid in his life.

"Honey, I can explain," he began, and her lips curled up in a snarl. He should have known better than to try that clichéd line. When she spoke, there was no warmth or love in her voice.

"Explain? And just what are you going to tell me, Sidney? The same old shit every man says to their wives when they get caught? It's been Yasmin Lewis all this time. How could I be so naïve?"

He knew there was little he could say, but he was willing to try.

"I am so sorry, honey. I have no excuses for what I did."

"No, you don't. How funny that you're counseling Sylvester Goodings after his wife left him for cheating on her. I guess it's easier giving advice than taking it."

"I'm not immune to sin, Livvy, even if I do preach the gospel. I've messed up, and I admit that, not only to God but to you. The vows I've made to you I broke, but honey, I'm asking for your forgiveness."

She merely looked at him as if he'd lost his damn mind.

"I can't believe this. You stand there and mouth platitudes as if all you did was forget my birthday. You slept with another *woman*! How the hell am I supposed to deal with that, especially after Tennessee when I thought things between us were getting better?"

"Baby, all I can say is I'm sorry. This has been gnawing at me for a long time."

"How *long?*" she demanded, and when he didn't answer, she just sighed.

"I can't trust you, Sidney. Nothing you're saying right now makes me want to trust you. You'll tell me anything I want to hear because a divorce would destroy everything you've built, and you don't want that."

Sidney hated to admit that she was partially right, but there were other considerations.

"What about the kids, Livvy? We shouldn't put them through that, not for a little indiscretion that will *never* happen again."

Olivia just shook her head incredulously, still holding his cell phone with all the incriminating evidence in her hand.

"*Now* you think about our children? Not while you were sexing up Yasmin Lewis? You were probably thinking about her while making love to me, so don't try to deny it. You know, this is all just too much for me to take right now."

She rose from the chair, and Sidney went to grab her hand but realized that his touch was probably the last thing she wanted from him.

"It would be best if you found someplace else to stay for a while, Sidney."

"You want me to leave?"

"Damn right I want you to leave!"

There was no hesitation in her voice.

"If you don't, *I* will. I will do two things. I'll keep this away from the children for now and keep this away from your mother, since she worships the damn ground you walk on. She'd somehow blame *me* for the reason you cheated. Now, get out!"

***

As he drove to the church, Sidney tried Yasmin's number several times, and each time, he had gotten her voicemail. He left messages but knew the chances of her returning them were slim.

She was still an addiction to him like a junkie needing his fix, and even though his marriage was close to laying in ruins, he still wanted her. He'd even had her even though she'd only turned to him out of desperation. At least there would be no one else since that Ambrose man had gotten an earful.

Pulling into the parking lot, he saw only one car near the back entrance. It was Ross's BMW, and Sidney groaned. Ross Tindal was the last person he wanted to see right now. Grabbing his weekender, he got out and headed to his office.

He could have gone to a hotel, but something led him here. He needed to think, to figure out if there was any way to save his marriage, his sanity, and of course, Holy Word. Yes, Olivia was upset. He couldn't blame her for that after everything between them in Tennessee.

A knock at the door of his office made him open his eyes.

"Come in."

Ross entered and quickly saw Sidney sitting in the dimly lit room. He looked around and his eyes fell on the weekender bag. He knew what happened.

"You finally got caught, didn't you, Sidney?"

There was no accusation, just a statement of fact. Sidney looked a little gray under the light of the desk lamp as he nodded.

"Can you believe that I left my phone, and Olivia found everything?"

It sounded ludicrous to his own ears, as if something so simple had tripped him up. Ross just shook his head.

"Maybe that was meant to happen."

Sidney sighed and leaned back in his desk chair.

"It still hasn't quite hit me, Ross. My marriage just might be over. I'm hoping and praying that Olivia will forgive me, if not for us, then for the sake of the kids."

Ross regarded his best friend and pastor unbelievingly.

"I wouldn't bet on it. Look what happened to Brother Goodings. He hasn't been the same since, and you were the one counseling him."

"I know all that," Sidney began, raising his voice.

"I was trying to forget Yasmin Lewis, but even when I was making love to my wife, I'd see her face. I feel like I'm obsessed with the woman or something."

He didn't tell Ross that they'd been together just hours ago. The other man walked toward the door.

"No, Sidney, you're not obsessed. You're just selfish, and you're going to lose everything that really matters. If your wife does forgive you, you'd damn well better get on your knees and thank, Jesus and then spend the rest of

204

your days making it up to her."

He left, closing the door quietly behind him.

***

Yasmin was lying in the middle of her living room, a broken woman. She felt so cold inside and so numb. No amount of water would ever wash away the sin and the stain of Sidney Teal, not for lack of trying. She didn't even understand why she gave in this last time. Maybe seeing the look of pain and betrayal on Ambrose's face had been too much. Maybe after that, she just didn't give a damn about anything.

I wonder who was the most surprised, him or me.

No amount of recrimination was going to erase the big fat mess she'd made of her life. *So much for moving on and leaving the past behind,* she thought sadly.

What would Ambrose do now? She wanted to call him back to explain and to confess. If he'd only given her the chance to tell her side of the story, that Sidney Teal didn't mean anything to her anymore.

Yeah right. Didn't April-Rose and Ronnie warn you that he'd already been dogged by one female? And here you go doing the same thing. She sighed. Would she always have to pay for her mistake? And what about

Sidney? What would the cost be to him? What would his wife do? Olivia Teal didn't look like the "stand by your man" type.

Yasmin grabbed her cell phone and speed dialed Ambrose's number. As she'd expected, it rolled over to voicemail, but she had to tell him the truth.

"Ambrose, I am so sorry that you saw and heard that, and you probably don't believe that it's been over between that man and me for a long time. I didn't even expect him to show up like that. Yes, it's true that I was having an affair with him before I met you, and—" She took a deep breath, trying to keep the tears at bay.

"Maybe I should have told you before anything got too serious between us, but I really thought I could leave that mess behind and start over with you. So much for that, right? I hope you'll call me, even if it's to say it's over. Maybe you'll give me another chance."

She was going to say more, but the tears she'd damned up broke through. She disconnected the call and just sobbed like an abandoned child.

***

Damn fool. You did it again. Ambrose managed to get a return flight back to L.A. that same day. It didn't even bother him that he'd had to pay extra. He just wanted out

206

of New York for good.

As he sat on the plane, he wondered sardonically just what it was about him and black women that was destined to fail and fail miserably. Maybe some of Ronnie's friends were right, that they wanted a thug and that nice guys with decent jobs were boring. Even women like Yasmin Lewis seemed to prefer being the dirty little secret to some married guy.

Ambrose didn't know what to do or what to feel. He really thought there could have been a chance between him and Yasmin, but perhaps not if she was keeping this a secret from him. How the hell would he have been able to trust her if this was still hanging over her?

Well, I guess that explained Ronnie's hesitation, he thought wryly. He wanted to call and curse his cousin out for not warning him, but then again, just maybe he didn't know about it.

Yeah right. Ronnie was one of those people who knew *everything,* and he was more than certain his girlfriend, April-Rose, knew, which meant *Ronnie* knew. But what would he have done anyway? Actually, it would have saved him a lot of money on phone calls, a round-trip ticket, and wondering if he was just a perpetual loser when it came to women.

When he finally arrived back home, he played Yasmin's message, giving it a careful listen as she tried to explain and apologize. Then, he erased it. Ambrose wished he could erase *her* out of his thoughts just as easily.

As he sat back, watching the sun fade into the sea from his redwood deck, he thought maybe he needed to hear from Yasmin what exactly had happened. But even if she told him the truth, how could he believe her? She might have said it was over, but for the man standing in her doorway, he obviously didn't get that text message.

When his cell phone rang, he saw it was Ronnie.

"Hey, cuz. What's going on?"

Ambrose just came right out.

"Tell me something. How much about Yasmin Lewis did you know before you and April-Rose set me up with her?"

"Oh shit."

The line went silent for several uncomfortable minutes.

"How did you find out?" Ronnie asked slowly.

"I flew out to New York to surprise her and ended up getting a rude surprise myself. Apparently, she'd been involved with a married man. Thanks for the heads up, cuz," he said sarcastically. He heard Ronnie swearing in the background and another voice which sounded like April-Rose's. When he came back to the phone, Ambrose heard the anger and the sorrow in his tone.

"Man, I don't know what to say. I thought—we both did—that she was over him. In fact, she made it clear it was over."

April-Rose's voice came through the receiver.

"Ambrose, I just wanted to give her a chance to start over again with a good man, and you two had a lot in common."

"And neither of you thought to mention her past to me after all the bullshit I'd already dealt with?"

Ronnie sounded defeated.

"I didn't think it mattered, but if it makes you feel any better, I hated not telling you."

"Yeah, I kind of had the feeling you were hiding something."

Ambrose took a sip of scotch.

"Well, it's over anyway, but the next damn time, stay the hell out of my love life."

***

Six weeks later, Yasmin sat in the OB/GYN waiting room, flipping through several magazines laid out on the small chestnut colored coffee table and wishing she hadn't eaten the bagel with cream cheese. Her period had been late, but she merely chalked that up to all the stress she'd been going through at work and at home. She seldom talked to April-Rose, who was still walking a thin line with her own boyfriend now that everything was out in the open.

She should have known the test would have come back positive for pregnancy. Of course, the only man she'd been with was Sidney Teal. Yasmin drove home in a haze.

CHAPTER SEVENTEEN

The last person April-Rose wanted to see was the woman who'd been more like a sister than a best friend. As she told Ronnie after the shit with Ambrose and Yasmin hit the fan, she loved Yasmin, but at the moment, she didn't like her very much. Ronnie was still playing phone and e-mail tag with Ambrose, trying to smooth things over out of a sense of guilt for getting his cousin all caught up in another woman's drama. Neither were thinking much about their upcoming wedding.

She let Yasmin into the living room. Her friend was quiet. April-Rose had a lot to say, but she swallowed her pride. Yasmin looked as if the world had run her over twice.

She sighed, her eyes full of regret.

"I am so sorry for getting you and Ronnie in the middle of all my mess. Girl, I don't know how many times you tried to tell me, and I really thought I was doing good and that Ambrose and I had a future together."

"You *did* have a future together," April-Rose said

boldly. "Was *he* really worth it?" she asked, meaning Sidney Teal. Yasmin looked directly at her friend.

"You already know the answer to that. On the other hand, it's what Sidney and I both deserve. I tried to forget it and to hide it, but as my grandma used to say 'God don't like ugly, and He ain't that keen on pretty either.'"

"So, now what?"

Yasmin sighed again, and the other woman's heart sank.

"I'm pregnant."

April-Rose's jaw dropped as she shook her head in complete disbelief.

"Shit! You don't do anything by halves, do you, Yaz? And I'm guessing the baby is *his*? The girl is about to get paid."

Yasmin nodded slowly.

"I'm going to tell him, but it's not about the money. I want Sidney to acknowledge this child."

Her friend rolled her eyes.

"Good luck with that. He's more concerned with that church of his, and he always has been. You were nothing more than a convenient hole to stick his dick in when wifey wasn't putting out."

Yasmin gasped, hearing the simmering anger in her

best friend's words and knowing they weren't meant to hurt but to force her to face her actions.

"Ronnie has been on the phone for the past few days, trying to make things right with his cousin, but he's not talking to anyone. I feel like I'm in the middle, and although Ronnie doesn't blame me, I feel kind of responsible for bringing you and Ambrose together."

"Maybe he'll forgive me someday. I think I was starting to fall for him, you know?"

April-Rose's eyes were filled with tears.

"Maybe. But you never loved *yourself*. If you had, you would have known from Jump Street that you were too good to be any man's piece of tail."

Just then, Ronnie came downstairs, saw Yasmin sitting there, and turned his head. The look on his dark brown features was as cold as ice. That made her feel even worse. How could this whole damn thing hurt so many innocent people?

"I warned you, Yasmin, about playing my cousin." Ronnie's voice was hard as was his stare.

"I can't believe you dogged him like that over that preacher man of yours. I don't know if you're stupid or just a triflin' ass bitch."

Yasmin and April-Rose gasped. Ronnie had never

spoken to her that way, but Yasmin accepted his rage stoically.

"April-Rose wanted better for you, and so did I, but I should have known you were never completely over Teal. I should have listened to my gut. After all, a woman who sleeps with a married man, especially when she *knows* he's married, is nothin' more than a nasty-ass hoe."

"Ronnie, you can't just blame her for this mess. Sidney Teal is just as much to blame." For God's sake, he's a man of the cloth. He knew better." April-Rose placed a comforting hand on her friend's shoulder.

"Yeah, but he didn't dog my cousin. *She* did."

"Look, I didn't know the man was coming over, and I didn't invite him," Yasmin said in her defense. "I told you I was done with him, and I meant that."

"Well apparently, he wasn't done with *you*," Ronnie spat.

"I guess his wifey wasn't puttin' out like she should, so he came over to get his freak on with a bitch who would."

"That's enough, Ron."

April-Rose sighed. Ronnie turned and left the room. Yasmin quietly walked out of the house, hoping and praying that *this* relationship wouldn't get caught up in all

214

her drama.

As she tossed and turned in bed that night, Ronnie's stinging words replayed in her mind. As long as she'd known him, he'd never said anything like that about any female, even though he'd known about her affair. He didn't like it and had told her in so many words, but this was the first time his real feelings had come out. Yasmin didn't hate him for it. After all, blood really was thicker than water.

***

For the first time since everything in her life had gone downhill faster than a snowball, Yasmin finally allowed herself to relax. Soaking in mimosa-scented bubbles, she thought of all the mistakes she'd made in her life, and if they weren't so stupid, they'd make for great drama.

"Maybe April-Rose is right, and I should sell my story to Lifetime," she said to herself. "Maybe some other woman can learn to do bad all by themselves."

There was very little she could do to make things right. She'd messed up so many lives, including her best friend's. April-Rose still had her back, but she'd made it clear that she was siding with Ronnie in their condemnation of what she'd done to Ambrose. They also blamed themselves.

Now there was a baby on the way. She would do right by the little life she carried within her. God had forgiven her. Of that, she was one hundred percent sure, but she now had to forgive herself and be a good mother to her child. Yasmin placed a wet hand on her abdomen, sure she could feel the heart beating within her. One of those things was to make damn certain that Sidney acknowledged his paternity and that the baby would know its brothers and sister. Why should it be held responsible for the sins of the parents? She didn't want or need Sidney's money. She never needed that, and she had the feeling that by the time his wife was done with him, he'd need the money more.

Revealing that he fathered a child on another woman would definitely spell the end of his career at Holy Word. Then again, maybe not. Yasmin had seen many times how church folks would forgive a man's indiscretions so easily, but not a woman's. Church women were especially bad about attacking each other in that respect. No wonder men like Sidney could get away with so much dirt.

***

It had taken every ounce of strength Olivia Teal possessed to maintain a somewhat united front for the children and for the church. All the while, she was making plans to leave and to take the kids with her.

Sidney tried his best, but his best just wasn't good enough anymore. She couldn't even look at him without feeling disgusted. She felt so foolish. All that advice she'd taken from Mother Teal when she should have been listening to her first mind. She'd so wanted things to be better. What wife didn't?

So many questions zipped through her mind. How long had he been cheating on her? Was Yasmin Lewis the only one, or were there other women at Holy Word who'd had a piece of him and walked around with airs, knowing that she was in the dark? One thing had been explained at least, his initial reluctance to have her on the Tennessee trip. He'd probably planned to have Yasmin join him there as she was certain he'd done in the past.

She cried her soul out when the kids were away and the house was quiet, for she'd made damn sure Sidney was nowhere around. She gazed at everything the two of them had built together over the years, and it just felt like an illusion. Everything she'd sacrificed to be the perfect wife, mother, and first lady of his church. It had been for nothing.

Every day she looked in the mirror and saw a

beautiful and proud woman any man would be happy to call wife. She kept a good home, took care of the children, and made the home a sanctuary. She honored her husband as scripture taught. No, she hadn't been perfect, but she'd thought herself pretty damn close. Was it because Yasmin Lewis was younger, more energetic, and had her own life and career? Was the sex better with her? Were there things Sidney wanted in bed that only Yasmin was willing to do? Olivia had read about kinky stuff that some folks were into. Maybe he was into that bondage or humiliation thing.

There was no one to talk to and no one she really trusted. Olivia's emotions wavered from despair to hatred and back and forth until she found herself taking an anxiety medicine just to steady her nerves and maintain some kind of balance. She had thought herself prepared for the eventuality and thought herself strong enough to handle it.

The last time he tried to talk to her, Olivia flew into a rage.

"I can't do this anymore, Sidney! I want a divorce!"

He looked absolutely stricken when she announced that, but she no longer cared.

"Every time I look at you, I just see Yasmin Lewis

218

and God knows how many other women. I can't live this way with a man I no longer love nor trust, and I don't want our children growing up in a home where there's discord.

"We can't lose it all, Livvy. Please give us one more chance."

Olivia closed her eyes. Tears escaped, despite her resolve.

CHAPTER EIGHTEEN

Yasmin took a sip of water and waited for the Teals to arrive. She made certain the booth she sat at was as close to private as possible.

It had all come to this moment. She might have lost Ambrose, but the baby she now carried would have some recognition. She'd make sure of that. She'd also make damn sure Sidney didn't walk away from this mess without scars.

The moment Olivia spied Yasmin Lewis, she wanted to turn around and drive far away from all the mess her husband and this woman had caused. On the other hand, she needed to hear the truth, and not from Sidney's lying mouth. Strangely enough, she felt nothing for the other woman; no hate, no pity, just nothing.

Sidney looked like a deer in the headlights. The day of reckoning had finally come upon him, but at least they were in a public place so there would be no *Maury* moments, at least not on *her* part. Olivia was far too classy a woman for such behavior.

"I'm glad you both came," Yasmin said, her voice steady and calm though her heart beat a mile a minute.

The waiter pulled out Olivia's chair, and she sat down with a dancer's grace. She was once again dressed to the nines in a dark blue Diane Von Furstenberg classic wrap dress and matching Blahnik heels. The sapphires in her ears and around her slender throat were elegant and understated, the way the woman herself was. She regarded Yasmin with curiosity.

Sidney simply plopped down in his chair and swallowed nervously. She'd never seen him so unsure or scared.

"Strange place for a meeting, Miss Lewis," Olivia said, eyes never leaving the younger woman's.

"Tell me something. Did you and my *husband* come here a lot?"

"I never went *anywhere* in town with him, Mrs. Teal. He didn't want his business out in the street."

"So why are we here, Miss Lewis? I'm sure it's not just for the food."

Olivia took a sip of white wine, wrapping her long elegant fingers around the stem of the wineglass. Yasmin instantly noticed the pale band around her finger where a wedding ring would usually sit. Olivia caught her gaze and smiled thinly.

"That's right. I'm no longer wearing my ring. It makes no sense really when it's just a piece of metal that, in the end, didn't mean a thing."

Yasmin took a warm roll from the linen-lined basket, broke it into two dainty pieces, and spread the soft unsalted butter on one half.

The other woman watched as the roll disappeared into Yasmin's mouth. She waited until she'd chewed then swallowed.

"I have a question that I'm sure so many women whose husbands have cheated on them have always wanted to ask the other woman. *Why?*"

Yasmin looked at Olivia unflinchingly.

"I was young, stupid, naïve, selfish, and thought I needed a man to be complete. That's what I was taught. I know better now. If it means anything to you, I'm truly sorry."

"No, my dear, your apology means *nothing* whatsoever," Olivia replied coldly.

"You and my cheating husband would have destroyed my life and that of my children if I allowed you to, but I won't."

Sidney felt a spark of hope. Hopefully, his marriage could be salvaged.

"Yasmin, can we please get to why we're here?" Sidney asked in a strained voice. "What do you want?"

"I am pregnant," Yasmin stated simply.

"The baby is Sidney's."

The air seemed to have left the room, and Sidney was left gasping for air.

"Are—are you sure? What about that Ambrose man you were seeing?"

Yasmin looked at Sidney like he was the lowest thing on the planet.

"No, Sidney, this baby is all *yours*. Ambrose and I have never been intimate, and after this, we never will be. I messed up and lost the best thing to have ever happened to me, but I won't let my baby grow up without knowing who her father is, and you *will* acknowledge her."

"What else do you want, Yasmin, child support?" Olivia asked sarcastically.

"Between what he's going to be paying me in alimony and support for his three children, there might not be a whole lot left, but you are certainly welcome to it."

"I don't need it," Yasmin replied with strength in her voice.

"This baby will be well taken care of financially, but I won't allow her to grow up thinking she's a bastard, and I want her to know her other brothers and sisters. The children shouldn't suffer for the foolishness of us adults."

Sidney gasped.

"How the hell am I supposed to explain who she *is*? They're just children, and they're too young to understand."

"You should have thought about *that* before you slept with *her*," Olivia pointed out acidly. "By the way..." She looked at Yasmin again. "How long were you and Sidney sleeping together? He made it sound as if it was just a one-time *mistake*."

Yasmin didn't even blink.

"Almost three years. I finally ended it around six months ago because I was tired of the whole thing. I wanted more from a relationship than Sidney could ever give me, and more importantly, I hated myself."

"Three years," Olivia repeated slowly as if in a trance.

"I've been living a lie for *three* whole years. My sons and my little girl have been calling this worthless lying son-of-a-bitch *Daddy* for three years, not knowing that he cared more about getting his freak on with you than about how he was hurting them."

Sidney tried to reach out to calm her, but she abruptly pulled away.

"Keep your cheating hands to yourself!"

"There's more. I had moved on with my life and even met someone wonderful who knew nothing about my past and cared for me with no strings. Unfortunately, what my mother always warned me about dirty deeds coming to light was true. He found out, and that was the end. I lost my mind, and well, the end result is *my* baby."

Olivia regarded her questioningly.

"You do realize what will happen to him at Holy Word once this gets out, right?"

Yasmin's gaze was steely.

"I really don't give a damn."

Olivia raised her glass in a mock toast.

"Neither do I. The way I see it, your terms are more than fair."

"Olivia," Sidney hissed, and she shot him a look so fierce that had it been daggers, he'd have been very dead.

Yasmin reached down and pulled a document from her Coach hobo bag.

"I had this drawn up by a discreet attorney friend of mine. It declares that Sidney Teal will acknowledge our child as his own by signing the birth certificate when she

225

is born, and the child will be treated like a member of Sidney Teal's own family."

"And if I don't sign?"

Sidney tried to call her bluff, but he wasn't ready for Olivia's response.

"Oh, you'll sign it all right," Olivia said. "For once in your miserable little life, do the right thing. You may have lost your church, you sure as hell have lost me and the children, but just maybe you can show everyone how a real man accepts his mistakes and tries to do better."

Utterly defeated, Sidney took out his black lacquered Montblanc and signed the paper as if he were signing in his own blood.

Olivia moved her chair back, stood up, and grabbed her purse.

"That's it then."

She took one last look at the young woman who'd once been her rival.

"Miss Lewis, I hope you teach your little girl better morals and better judgment than you yourself have shown. I am sorry that you lost a second chance, but you brought it upon yourself."

Yasmin carefully folded the paper and placed it into her bag. She sighed resignedly.

"I know, and I fully accept the consequences of my actions."

"Olivia, where are you going?"

Sidney stood up, but she waved him away.

"*I* am going home. I don't really care *where* you go. Maybe you should take a trip to Brother Goodings and keep him company."

Sidney watched her walk out the door, unable to move, to call her back, or to apologize. He did not see Yasmin leave either. Holding a glass of wine in his hand, he downed it in one swallow. Like his life now, it tasted bitter. He'd lost it all for vanity, for greed, and for lust.

What a hell of a sermon that would make, he thought ironically.

EPILOGUE – ONE YEAR LATER

Pastor Ross Tindal straightened his robes one last time as his beaming wife, Chantel, grinned from the side, holding their bubbly two-year-old, Marleena. His stomach was a little jittery, but as he closed his eyes in a quick prayer, he felt the spirit of the Lord enter him, and suddenly, whatever nervousness or unsurety he'd felt dissipated like fog.

"I can't believe this is really happening, honey," he said as they clasped hands, still as much in love as they'd ever been. So much had happened over the past year in their lives, from the painful discovery that he'd been sterile since birth, the adoption of their daughter, the downfall and scandal surrounding his best friend and former pastor, Sidney Teal, to the shocked announcement that Yasmin Lewis had borne him a daughter she'd named Amber-Lynn. All of it had felt like a freight train gone crazy.

As Chantel had warned him, most of the resentment fell upon Yasmin who was viewed uncharitably as the homewrecker by a fairly large portion of the female congregation. Sidney was viewed as the poor man tempted by the sinful woman. Olivia Teal also did not

228

escape unscathed. It had shocked Ross to hear that some in the church thought that she should have remained married and steadfast even in the face of infidelity. As some had put it, "men will always be dogs," which just seemed like a sad excuse.

After stepping down, Sidney packed his bags. Watching him, he seemed less larger than life and older.

"You warned me," he said as he placed his worn bible into a suitcase.

"You warned me, Ross, and as Mama used to tell me, I didn't believe that fat meat's greasy. God will not be mocked, my brother. You best believe that."

"So what now, Sidney?"

The older man looked weary but still managed a slight smile.

"Back home for now. Olivia and I are trying to make this divorce as easy on the kids as possible, but they all still cry at night because they don't understand why Daddy is going away for a while."

Ross didn't want to ask, but Sidney appeared to read his thoughts.

"Yes, I'm keeping my agreement with Yasmin, so the kids know Amber-Lynn is their sister. Ironically, Amia likes having the baby around."

With the last of his personal items packed, Sidney took one last look at everything he'd built and sighed sadly.

"Not much left to say, is there, Pastor Tindal? Love your wife and cherish her. You've seen two men brought down by lust and selfishness, and you've seen so many lives in ashes. I have indeed reaped the whirlwind, and it pains me to hear some in the church try to blame Olivia and Yasmin. As I said before, God will not be mocked."

Chantel placed a comforting hand on her husband's arm, bringing him back to the present.

"Well, it is, and you're more than ready."

Before he opened the door of the office, he took his wife into his arms, careful not to squish Marleena, who gazed at her daddy with the trusting eyes of a child. He kissed Chantel quickly but passionately.

"I love you so much," he said and meant every word.

"I love you too, Ross Tindal. Now, you get out there and rock Holy Word," she replied with a saucy wink.

"Amen!"

THE END

Do not be deceived:
God cannot be mocked.
A man reaped what he sows.

Galatians 6:7

QUESTIONS FOR DISCUSSION

1) Do you think relationships such as Sidney's and Yasmin's exist in churches today?

2) If the church members had found out about the affair between them, how would they have reacted?

3) Do you think we tend to view leaders of God as infallible?

4) What do you think made Pastor Sidney fall from grace?

5) Do you think he was truly committed to his calling?

6) If you were Olivia would you have forgiven him for his affair?

7) What do you think of women like Yasmin Lewis?

8) What do you think of Pastors like Pastor Sidney Teal?

ACKNOWLEDGEMENTS

Once again, I would like to give praise to my Lord and Savior Jesus Christ for allowing me to take this journey yet again. I would like to give thanks to my family and friends for their love and ongoing support. I dedicate this novel to all my grands, especially my newest one, Little R.J. To everyone, I say believe in your dreams, no matter how long they may take. It's worth waiting for.

I would love to hear from you.

http://sweetsmells2003.wixsite.com/janie-decoster

Twitter: @JanieDecoster

Face Book: Janie De Coster

BIO

My love of writing began in my high school years with poetry. It wasn't until many years later that I heard a spiritual voice instructing me to write a book. Having no idea as to what genre it would be, I just put pen to paper.

Over the years, I have penned several genres; romantic suspense, women's fiction, contemporary, and paranormal through a previous publisher. I am the author of *The Sisters Series: What My Sister Didn't Know* book 1 and 2 which have been on the Amazon Best Sellers list and featured in several magazines such as *SHE Mag*, *Urban Lit* and *Pen Ashe Magazine*.

I write not only to entertain but to educate as my topics shine a light on issues of today's society such as mental illness, domestic violence, infidelity, and low self-esteem. In my spare time, I like to travel, shop, and spend quality time with my husband, children, and grandchildren.

Be sure to LIKE our Major Key Publishing

page on Facebook!

CPSIA information can be obtained
at www.ICGtesting.com
Printed in the USA
LVHW05s2334080618
580208LV00008B/159/P